The Keeper's Secret

Tell-Tale Publishing's Annual Horror Anthology

Tell-Tale Publishing's Annual Horror Anthology, 2016

Tell-Tale Publishing Group, LLC
5714 Peri St.
Swartz Creek, MI 48473
www.tell-talepublishing.com

Foreword

Whether it's history itself getting lost in the stone silence of a lighthouse or the time flow of medieval armor clashing from the grave into the now of your mind, this year's honor roll of top stories from Tell-Tale Publishing will pull you up in your chair and set your pulse racing. But that's what you want…isn't it? There will be thoughtful dilemmas to keep you pondering, moral choices and choices for the oldest of reasons – love – and above all the test of love versus fate. Nowhere will fate be more exquisitely tangled than in the tale of a young woman trapped between the terror of sexual abuse and the unknowns in the magical world of the Jinn. And just as you think you've felt it all from rescues and would-be rescues each twisted with karma, steel yourself for one more. Because the perfect ending might be a perfect day whose ironies will jolt you as you stare into a psychological mirror. So find that chair and open this book. You won't be putting it down for a while.

Thomas Sullivan

USA Today best-selling author of CASE WHITE

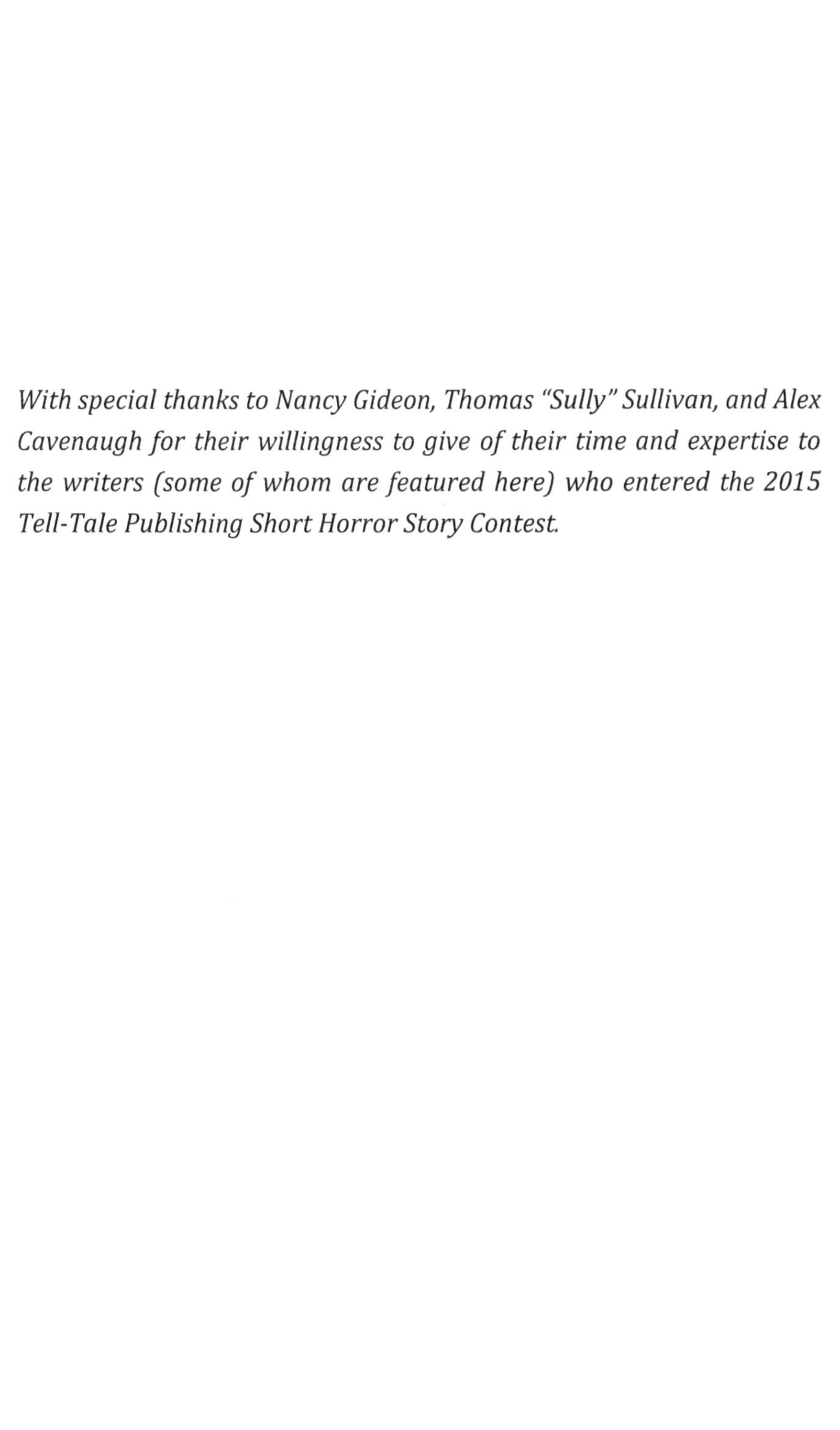

With special thanks to Nancy Gideon, Thomas "Sully" Sullivan, and Alex Cavenaugh for their willingness to give of their time and expertise to the writers (some of whom are featured here) who entered the 2015 Tell-Tale Publishing Short Horror Story Contest.

Table of Contents

The Keeper's Secret

Robert James

**Winner of Tell-Tale's 2015
Vincent Price Award**

He stared at her.

They always stared.

That's how she knew he was dead.

Megan stopped short of the front entrance to the Shawnee Point Lighthouse and looked at the reflection in the window. He stood by the rocks in the shadow of the lighthouse tower, staring. Even with the glare of the sun obscuring his face, she could feel his cold, searching eyes unpacking her soul, memorizing her deepest secrets.

"Megan, let's go," her father said. "Shawnee Point is one of the tallest on the lakes. You can see Wisconsin from up there!" He opened the door and fanned the air impatiently.

When Megan turned to get a better look at the man, he was standing inches from her face. Before she could react, he grabbed her by both arms. She hated this part most of all. For an instant, Megan's body turned inside out, her entire existence laid bare for the dead man's inspection. He released his hands, severing their link. Megan took a deep breath and exhaled slowly, caught up in the power of his hazy, charcoal eyes. Finding her legs, she turned and walked through the door.

"I'm going to grab a water," her dad said, oblivious. "I'll meet you up there." He pointed to a set of circular stairs before disappearing into an adjacent room.

She knew he meant well, but the torture started right after her mom died. "You have to live history, Megan," her dad preached that first summer. "It's not something you just read about in books. These are real places. They were real people."

They were real all right. Megan had been bringing them home as souvenirs ever since.

She hit the stairs, her feet pounding a steady cadence against the wrought iron steps as she climbed higher and higher into the sky. When she emerged from the stairway into the crisp, autumn breeze, he was waiting for her. He stood with his hands on the railing, watching the rich blue waters of Lake Michigan meet the rocky shore over a hundred feet below. His immaculate black uniform complemented his black hair and handsome features. He looked like he had just walked out of a portrait.

They always did.

"What's your name?" Megan asked.

"Joseph," he replied.

"So, what's your story, Joseph?"

Joseph reached out and took Megan's hands, sending a fresh surge of raw energy all the way to her toes. He pushed the sleeve of her blouse up past her wrist, revealing the technicolor tattoo intended to hide her botched suicide. He clamped his thumb over her scar, and looked into her eyes. Megan felt him penetrate deep into the shadows of her heart, her wrist burning with the heat of his touch. *Oh, shit.*

"Wait, I…" Megan gasped, but she wasn't able to finish.

Joseph wrapped her tightly in his arms, and sprang from the tower, sending them both head over heels toward the rocks below. Pulsing with adrenaline, Megan screamed all the way down, until she and Joseph met the earth with a sudden jolt, and everything went black.

Megan shuddered and grabbed the guardrail. As her senses returned to normal, she did her best to shake off Joseph's greeting. She knew better. Lost souls always acted on their instincts when they first met her. When Joseph felt her scar, it was like an open invitation to take a flying leap.

"Megan, you okay?" her dad asked. "Hey," he gave her a nudge on the shoulder, "that's a lot of steps, eh?" He was a large man, and the stairs had clearly had their way with him.

"Yeah, no," Megan replied, "I'm fine. No worries."

"This is total bullshit," he said, exasperated. "You can't see fucking Wisconsin from here." Her dad had been a prolific curser as long as Megan could remember. "Hey, buddy," he said to a man a few feet away, "can you see Wisconsin?" The man shook his head.

"Tell me about it," Megan said, "fucking tourist trap." He might have rubbed off on her. "You gonna' get our money back?" she asked, playing along.

"Nah, it was free." He opened his bottle of water and took a sip, then put his arm around Megan's shoulders. "I know it's just across town, but you don't turn seventeen every day. Happy seventeenth, Meg."

"Thanks, dad." Megan rested her head on his thick shoulder. Joseph was standing on the rocks below, right where they had landed, staring up at Megan and her dad. He waved. She smiled back and sighed. Dead people were so annoying.

***

No matter what she did, Megan knew that Joseph would be with her for the next couple of days. She learned that lesson early. Not letting the dead lady into her dad's car was the first thing she thought of when she was seven years old. Megan burst into tears that day when the wrinkled old prune was waiting in their driveway two hours later. She sat at the kitchen table while Megan ate dinner, her pale, wrinkled face stuck in neutral. Later that night, she stood at the foot of Megan's bed, staring through the darkness as she tried to sleep. Two days later, when Megan found her standing next to the corn niblets in the pantry, she finally mustered the courage to say hello. The woman's gurgling attempt at a reply sent Megan screaming into the front yard and down the street.

Since then, she had made a point to linger with the car door open for a few extra seconds, so her new friend had time to sit down. There was no sense dragging things out, and besides, the ride home gave them extra time to get all of the staring out of the way. Even though the lighthouse was only 15 minutes from their house, by the time they got home, Joseph was almost ready to have a conversation.

She led him into her bedroom, shut the door and pointed at the chair by her desk. Joseph walked to the chair and sat down. Megan grabbed the journal from her nightstand, and sat down on her bed. *A Teenager's Guide to Assisting Lost Souls, by Megan Worthington*, was scrawled across the front cover. She started the journal when she was at Lakepointe Hospital. It was part of her therapy, designed to help her explore the many faces and personalities she 'claimed' to interact with.

Her therapist at Lakepointe was a royal douche. Most days, she came to the hospital hungover, and counted the minutes until her shift was over (literally, and out loud). Megan had to try to work with her, though, or she might still be in that shithole. She couldn't imagine being the only person in the world who hung out with dead people, so she started the journal with some good, sound advice.

What Makes a Lost Soul Annoying:
1. *They stare. Especially when you first meet them. Rude.*
2. *They only know their name. The rest is up to you. Dumb as fucking rocks.*
3. *If you show a lost soul a picture of themselves while they were alive, a dark swirling hole will swallow the*

picture and they will vomit uncontrollably. Thick, black, smelly, nasty vomit.

4. *If a lost soul vomits in your presence, you will also vomit uncontrollably.*

5. *In general, you will lose control of your bodily functions while hanging out with dead people. Don't worry, it's perfectly natural to piss yourself under these circumstances. This is some freaky shit.*

6. *UNDER NO CIRCUMSTANCES, should you EVER take a lost soul to a cemetery. Bad things will happen. <u>Very bad things!</u>*

Over time, she had added to the list as she made new friends with new needs. Megan grabbed her pen, and set the journal on her lap. *7. Avoid high places for the first 24 hours*, she wrote. She had a separate chapter in her journal for each lost soul she had met over the years. *#42: Joseph*, she wrote at the top of the next blank page.

"Hi, Joseph," Megan said, looking up from her journal.

"Hi, I…I…d…d…do," Joseph stuttered.

"It's okay," Megan said, smiling. "In a little while, you'll be able to talk. I need to help you remember a few things first. Just chill here for a minute, okay? I'm going to grab a book that might help." She hopped up from her bed, and walked out into the living room. Her dad was tucking into a beer and starting an episode of *Ancient Aliens* he had on the DVR.

"Can I borrow that book you bought at the lighthouse?" she asked.

"Knock yourself out," he pointed absently. "It's over on the kitchen table. What the fuck is with that guy's hair?" he pointed at the TV, shaking his head.

She retrieved the book and kissed the top of his shiny bald head. "You're just jealous. Goodnight, dad," she said, trotting back to her bedroom. Megan was surprised to find Joseph was still sitting on the chair at her desk, as instructed. He smiled and waved as she walked into the room. *He listens well*, she thought, *my favorite kind*. Flopping down on her bed, she looked at her new charge. He was handsome by any measure, even with an opaque complexion and discolored teeth. He was thin, but clearly athletic, and his mop of thick black hair begged to be mussed. *Damn.*

Megan cleared her throat and opened up the book to the table of contents. It was a history of the Shawnee Point Lighthouse, organized by decade. She wasn't sure when Joseph died, so she opted for the index, which was useless without a last name. "Joseph," she said, looking up from the book, "my name is Megan. Megan Worthington." She emphasized her last name, saying it slowly, hoping he would take the hint.

"Joseph," he said, "Joseph F…F…Foster."

Megan's finger traced a path through the book's index. "Well, you're in here, Joseph. Just one page, but you're here." Megan flipped to the referenced page and started reading aloud.

A Dark History

The Shawnee Point Lighthouse was constructed in 1877, during the heyday of sail on the Great Lakes. In addition to being the tallest lighthouse, it also has a more deadly distinction. Two different lake currents converge on the shoals offshore, and are the final resting place for seventy-eight shipwrecks and over three-hundred sailors. The lighthouse's first keeper, Joseph Foster, a distinguished hero from the Evanston Lifesaving Station, fell to his death in a storm during its first season of operation.

Megan stopped reading and looked at Joseph to see if anything was registering. He blinked – then stared – so she continued reading.

During the 1920s, the Army Corps of Engineers dynamited a large section of the shoal, making navigation safer. But even this was not without tragedy, as the salvage tug used for the operation exploded when a fire broke out, killing all eighteen men aboard.

"Joseph Foster," he said, "I…I was a light keeper." He looked at Megan from across the room.

"That's it, Joseph, keep trying," she said without looking up from the book. *That's it?* There was nothing else in the entire book about Joseph, and no details about his accident. Megan's senses were tingling. There had to be more. She had learned the hard way that historians liked to leave out messy details that didn't fit their neat little narrative, but details were critical for helping lost souls move on. She needed more.

Megan grabbed her meds out of her pill box and swallowed them down, then spent a few minutes scratching down notes into her journal. "Goodnight, Joseph," she said, turning off the light. She heard Joseph stand up and walk over to her bed. Even with her head buried under the pillow, she could feel the weight of his stare, inches from her face. "Go back and sit down on the chair, Joseph," she said through her pillow, "it's not polite to stare in the dark." A few minutes later, her sleeping pill worked its magic, and she was sound asleep.

***

The next morning, Megan woke to find Joseph sitting on the chair, staring at the wall. *He listens VERY well,* she thought.

"Good morning, Joseph," she said, putting a brush through her artificially colored purple hair. She grabbed a band and put her hair up into a tight pony tail, exposing her shaved neck and another tattoo that ran from her hairline down onto her back. In an instant Joseph was on her, wide-eyed and reaching. "No," Megan said, slapping her hands over the tattoo. "No more touching, Joseph. We need to learn how to talk to each other. It's the only way you're going to figure this out. Trust me."

He took a few steps back.

"That's better," she said. "I have to go do some research at the library this morning." She applied her mascara and a thick bead of eye liner, followed by blood red lipstick. "It's best if you stay here, Joseph. I bet looking at this book will help you. Are you willing to try for me?" she asked, setting it on the desk next to him. He nodded his head.

At this stage, lost souls were still predictable. She figured he would be able to start forming sentences by the time she got back. It was after they started talking coherently that you had to be careful, because that meant they were starting to think. Depending on their personality, a lost soul's thoughts lead to actions that were anything from hilarious to terrifying.

Megan grabbed a granola bar to eat on the way to the library. It was after 9AM, so her dad had been gone for nearly three hours. He wouldn't let Megan get a job, and they agreed she would wait a year before starting at the community college. Helping Joseph was officially all she had to do. She pulled on her running shoes and walked out the door. She never left home without her running shoes. Megan believed that tall boots were the work of the devil, and only worn by prostitutes. She could barely walk in heels, and she certainly couldn't run away from dead people in them. Her running shoes were the only thing that kept her 'athletic yet chunky' frame from becoming just chunky.

Their house was about halfway down the dead-end street. With its baby blue siding, it begged for attention next to white, off-white, and dirty white neighbors. Megan walked down the sidewalk toward the grove of trees where the street ended at a metal guardrail. A trail through the woods led to the railroad tracks, and then on into Lakepointe, a shortcut to mischief that Megan had used since she was old enough to go outside alone.

When she arrived at the library, Megan found her way over to the microfiche readers and the cabinets filled with early newspapers. A reference librarian helped her find two microfilms from the summer of 1877. She fed the first one into the machine, and started flipping through. It took her about an hour, and four more rolls of film, before she found something useful. It was an article written up in the society section. Apparently there had been a debutante ball at a dance hall just down the beach from the lighthouse. The couples of honor had all been photographed, with a short caption under each.

Joseph Foster and Angeline Hudson

Mr. Foster, with fiancée Angeline Hudson of Southwood, is the light keeper at the new Shawnee Point Lighthouse, a sorely needed and much anticipated aid to shipping and commerce in the region. Mr. Foster comes from the Evanston Lifesaving Station, where he is credited with saving the lives of over 150 men, women and children when the passenger steamer Pawtucket capsized offshore.

Megan looked at the picture. Joseph had a broad smile and a confident look on his face. He was wearing a tuxedo that was cut exceptionally close to his chiseled torso. Well, Megan imagined it was a chiseled torso. He was some kind of hero, after all. She flipped ahead, scanning through the remaining film in the reader to no avail. She needed to find out more about how he died. With a yawn, she loaded up the next film from the summer of 1877.

It only took a couple of minutes to find what she was looking for. The accidental death of the hero of Evanston made front page news. There was a long, drawn out obituary, celebrating his kindness, bravery, and kindness to small animals, but it was a sentence at the end of the article that got Megan's attention. *The news of this tragedy is especially hard for Miss Hudson, as it was a picturesque evening, with dry conditions, and the lake flat calm.* Megan smiled, her suspicion confirmed. Joseph's death was no accident.

***

Megan flopped down on the couch with a diet soda and told Joseph about what she had found at the library.

"Angeline," Joseph said. "I remember." A tear ran down his cheek. "I can see her in my mind, laughing and smiling. What's love?"

"Love," Megan said, "that's a strong word." She felt a twinge of jealousy. "Love is a feeling, Joseph. Sometimes it's strong, and sometimes it's more like a whisper. It can be happy, like your feelings for Angeline, but it can also be sad, like when you can't be with the person you love."

"Did you love your mother?"

"Of course I loved her," Megan snapped. She didn't know why Joseph asked her that. Every lost soul she had ever met knew that the instant they touched her. "Tell me about Angeline," she redirected. "What do you remember?"

"Her hair smelled like flowers," he said, "and her eyes were always so happy. I remember her lips. They were soft and warm, and her body…"

"Okay, that's great, Joseph!" Megan interrupted. She didn't know why she was jealous of a dead woman, but it didn't matter, in a day or two Joseph's pasty face would be just another fading memory in her journal. "So, what do you remember about the lighthouse?"

"Fog." He looked at Megan and blinked, wide-eyed. "I remember fog."

Megan could tell that Joseph's mind was waking up, but it was no use asking him about how he died. He wasn't ready yet. She took a hit of her diet soda, and started checking her text messages.

***

"Hey, dad," Megan said, as they ate dinner that night. "Do you remember seeing anything about Joseph Foster at the lighthouse? He was the first light keeper there." She took a bite of meatloaf.

"No, can't say I do."

"Exactly," Megan said. "You'd think the first light keeper would have a display or something, right? Turns out he was pretty famous, some kind of hero. Here, take a look at this." Megan pulled out a copy of the picture she had made at the library. Joseph was safely on the other side of the room, watching them eat.

"Huh, how about that," her dad said, looking absently at the photo, and taking a drink of water.

"Yeah, he died his first summer on the job," Megan continued, "fell off the tower and smashed onto the rocks. Probably fell right from where we were standing yesterday." Megan gave Joseph a dirty look and speared a carrot.

"No kidding," her dad said, "that *is* messed up. No wonder they didn't have a display or anything." His interest now piqued, he picked the photocopy back up and gave it another look, reading the caption. "Angeline Hudson. Why does that name sound familiar?

Wait a minute," he said, getting up from the table. "I'll be right back." He came back with an overflowing white binder and flipped through the pages until he found what he was looking for. "Check this out, Meg," he said, smiling.

Megan looked at the paper he had pulled from the binder. It was a family tree worksheet. He pointed to a name in the upper left corner. "Here, see that? Angeline Hudson. She married Augustus Worthington in 1882." He poked Megan in the shoulder. "Those are our people, Meg. She was your great-great-grandmother."

"Are you fucking kidding me?" Megan stood up from the table. She had never brought home a lost soul that was even remotely related to her family or anyone she knew. Joseph stood up, sensing Megan's surprise. She grabbed the photo off the table and folded it back into her pocket.

"That is so cool," her dad said. "I never came across anything about that in the family history stuff."

"Probably because she didn't want people to know about it, just like the white-washed history in that book you bought." Megan looked again at the family tree. "What do you mean?"

"The book says he died accidentally during a storm, but the newspaper article I found said the night was dry and the lake was flat calm." Megan looked at her dad. "I think it was a suicide."

The word struck her dad square in the face. He stared with his mouth open for a split-second before regaining his composure. "No, I'm sure there is a perfectly normal explanation for what happened," he said, "there always is."

Megan didn't believe that for a second.

***

Megan was scratching some more notes into her journal when she heard her dad start talking. He rarely talked to anyone on his phone, and never this late at night. Something was wrong. She tiptoed down the hallway, and pressed her ear against his bedroom door.

"…a problem…yes," she heard him say, "she spent the day at the library doing some research on the guy…yeah, the lighthouse outside of town… it was an accident, but she used the word suicide…yes, she's even been writing about it in her journal."

Bastard, Megan thought, *you promised me you wouldn't read it anymore.* Joseph came over to the door, his face inches from hers. He looked at Megan and blinked. "Go away!" she mouthed without speaking. He pressed his ear against the door and frowned, imitating Megan's scowl.

"…I know, but she's been so solid the past six months," her dad said. "You know she won't want to go back…alright, I'll put on some coffee…see you in a bit…right, bye."

Shit! Dr. Jennings was coming over. Megan padded quickly down the hallway. "Come on!" she mouthed at Joseph, waving her hand. The last time Dr. J. made a house call, they put her into Lakepointe, and it effed everything up with Orrin, the little boy she brought home from a museum in Chicago. This would make her progress with Joseph go to shit in a hurry. Still in her pajamas, she grabbed her purse, her tennis shoes, and a sweatshirt and headed quickly to the back door.

"Come on, Joseph," she whispered, "we have to go!" She opened the door and waited for him to get through before gently closing it behind her. Once she was outside, she ran hard down the sidewalk into the night. Two houses down the street, a rock gouged her heel. She half-shouted in pain and ducked behind a shrub. She put on her shoes and laced them as fast as she could. She looked back down the street. She didn't see her dad, so she started running again.

At the end of her street, Megan and Joseph ducked into the woods to follow the trail downtown. She slowed to a walk, pulled out her cell phone from her purse, and punched a few numbers. A groggy voice grumbled hello.

"Justin, I need you to meet me in the alley behind O'Malley's," she said, "And bring your car."

"Hello to you too. You know what time it is, right? What's going on, Megan? You sound out of breath."

"No time to explain. Just meet me there – now!" She put her phone back into her purse, and started running again. When she emerged from the woods, she and Joseph kept to the shadows until she got to O'Malley's. Crouching behind a dumpster, she put on her sweatshirt and waited for Justin to arrive. Her phone started buzzing in her purse. Her dad was calling her. *Hurry up,* she texted Justin.

Where are you? her dad texted.

You promised! How could you! Megan replied.

Come home Meg – where are you?

Megan ignored the text, and gave her dad the cyber-silent treatment. A few minutes later, a green Ford Taurus rumbled into the alley and the passenger side window rolled down. Megan turned off her phone and stood up.

"Nice outfit," Justin said, eyeing her pajama bottoms, "hop in."

"No," Megan replied, "get out of the car. I need to get away for a while. Alone."

"What the fuck, Megan?" Justin replied. "You know I can't do that."

"You promised. At Lakepointe, you promised. You told me that if I ever needed something, all I had to do was say the word. Are we adding liar to your resume, you murdering, bi-polar piece of shit?" Megan sneered. If she hadn't vouched for him that night, he'd probably be in prison. The nurse he beat up was in a coma for three months before her husband pulled the plug.

"Fuck you!" Justin replied. He pounded his fist against the dashboard. "Damnit, Megan!" He shook his head, mumbled something to himself, then opened the door and stepped out of the car.

Megan opened the front passenger door and gestured at Joseph. She waited until he was in the car before closing the door and walking to the driver's side. Justin rolled his eyes as she got behind the wheel. He didn't believe in ghosts, but he knew all about her friends. "There isn't much gas. I want it back by Friday with a full tank," he said, banging on the window. "Don't do anything stupid!"

She hit the gas and roared away without responding.

***

Megan didn't know where she was going, but she needed to put some distance between herself and a one-way ticket back to Lakepointe Hospital. Hopefully she would be able to figure this out quickly and help Joseph move on. "We're going away for a little while, okay, Joseph? I can't explain, but you need to trust me. Do you trust me?" Joseph nodded his head. "Good," she smiled.

She drove out of town as far as she could before stopping for gas. She pulled into a pump, and reached instinctively into her purse for her debit card. *Shit,* Megan thought. She wouldn't be surprised if her dad had already called the police. If she used the card, they could trace her location. She dug through her purse and found a $5 bill. This was not going well. She looked at the clerk inside. "Pre-pay or card after 10 pm, pump seven," he said dryly over the intercom.

Her mind raced, trying to think of a way to make $50 magically appear. She took off her sweatshirt and threw it in the front seat, then walked toward the cash register. This was so below her, she hated herself for even thinking of it. When she got inside, she ran her hand through her hair, and flipped it back over her shoulder. "Oh, shit," she said, pretending to dig through her purse. "I left my debit card at home, and all I have is $5. Is there any way you can help me out tonight? I promise I'll come back tomorrow and pay you." She bit her lip and gave the clerk her best pouty face, leaning over the counter so her breasts could say hello.

"Right," he said, clearly annoyed, "you think you're the first girl to try that? So, that will be five dollars on pump seven, then?" He held out his hand without waiting for a reply. Megan folded her arms across her chest and gave him the middle finger before slapping the $5 bill on the counter.

"Tell him Carla says hello," Joseph said into her ear. Megan didn't even notice he was standing next to her. She looked at him, confused. "Say it," he insisted.

Megan turned to the clerk. "Carla says hello."

The clerk's eyes got wide and his face went pale. "What did you just say?"

"Carla says hello?"

"How do you know about her? What is this? Why are you here?" The clerk stood up from his chair and started rocking back and forth on his feet.

"Tell him you're going to tell the police how he shoved her in a bag and dumped her in the big lake if he doesn't give you fifty dollars on pump seven," Joseph said.

"What the *fuck,* Joseph?" Megan turned to face him, unable to hide her horrified surprise.

"Who's Joseph?" the clerk asked. "Look, you need to get out of here, right now!"

Megan looked at the clerk with a new level of disgust. "No," she said firmly, "you need to give me fifty dollars on pump seven, or I'm going to tell everyone how you dumped her in the lake!" Megan pounded the counter with her fist for good measure.

"Alright, alright," the clerk said, punching some buttons, "please, I didn't mean to hurt her. It was an accident. I didn't know what to do."

"Shut up, you twisted fuck," Megan said, fully accepting the role Joseph had provided. She grabbed some diet soda, a couple bags of chips and some beef jerky on her way to the door. "I was never here," she said, pushing the door open with her hip and shuffling away as fast as her overloaded arms would allow.

As she drove away with a full tank of gas, she cracked open the diet soda and gave Joseph a wide-eyed look, and asked, "What was that?"

"We needed gas," Joseph said, blinking.

"Don't you blink at me, Joseph Foster," Megan retorted, "you're way past the blinking stage. How did you know about that girl, Carla?" she asked.

"All three of the people he killed were there at the gas station. I just picked the one that would help us get what we needed."

"That guy killed three people?"

"Two women and one little girl," Joseph said.

"Which one was Carla?" Megan asked, chills running up her neck.

Joseph looked at her and blinked.

***

Megan followed the two-lane highway out of town until the light from Shawnee Point came into view. Even from the highway, Megan could see it sending its signal out into the darkness. She turned onto a county road, and drove up into the hills away from the shore. When she saw the entrance to a small park, she pulled in and found a spot to rest. The park was up on a bluff, and they could see all the way down to Lake Michigan. It was a calm night, and the reflection of the nearly full moon shimmered like glass across the dark water.

"So, do you remember anything about the lighthouse yet?" Megan asked. She thought looking out at the water might help.

"No, just fog," Joseph replied. "I don't know why, but every time I try to think about the lighthouse, or my life there, I get the same image – fog." He frowned at Megan.

"We're getting there, Joseph," Megan said. "You're having conversations now, so it shouldn't be long before we jog your memory. I want to take you back to the lighthouse. It should help get things set straight, but I'm fried. I really need some rest first." She looked out the windshield, her eyes heavy. She was just drifting off to sleep when Joseph started talking again.

"Doesn't this hurt?" He flicked the piercing in her right nostril with his finger.

"Get your moldy paw out of my face, and let me go to sleep!"

"Do you miss your mom?" he asked.

"Fuck off, Joseph," Megan said without opening her eyes. She was just drifting off to sleep again, when he asked, "why did you try to kill yourself?"

"Why do you keep asking me questions you already know the answer to?" She let out an exasperated groan and turned her shoulder away from him in protest.

"Because I want to hear you say the words. Sometimes what you think and feel can change, you know," Joseph said, poking her in the shoulder with a pale finger.

Megan's blue eyes narrowed and turned to ice. "Partly because I wanted to be with my mom, and partly because I'm tired of helping annoying fucking dead people like you!" She got out of the car and slammed the door behind her. "Fuck you, Joseph!" she shouted through the windshield. She slammed her fist on the hood of the car and sulked away.

Why is he bugging me with bullshit questions? In some ways, Joseph was just like every other lost soul she had ever helped cross over, but in other ways he was completely new. She had never met a dead person she was almost related to, and she had never had to explain herself to any of them. It was like Joseph was doing it on purpose, a big brother teasing his little sister for a cheap thrill.

Something rustled in the trees. At first Megan thought it was the wind, but as she listened more closely, it resembled whispering voices. She ran up the hill next to the parking area, then stopped dead in her tracks. On the other side of the rise was row after row of tombstones. Megan turned and ran back toward the car. "Joseph! We have to go!" she cried, but he was gone.

"Joseph….Joseph…" a husky, mocking voice materialized around her. The voice seemed to come from everywhere and nowhere all at once. "Hey," the voice rumbled. Megan spun around to find an enormous beast of a man standing directly in front of her. He wore black coveralls with no shirt and was layered in mud from head to toe. He was bald, with thick cheeks and a pug nose. Behind him were six equally large companions, some carrying shovels, while others had pick axes and lanterns. "How did you escape?" he asked, planting his giant hand on her shoulder.

"We have to put you back into the ground, little one." He snorted and spit on the dirt by Megan's feet. Without thinking, she lashed out at his face, gouging his eyes with her fingers.

The man threw her down, and the others swarmed, binding her arms and legs and stuffing her mouth full of grass and debris. When Megan could no longer put up a struggle, the man hoisted her over his shoulder and walked up the slope into the tombstones. He stopped at a particularly impressive, obelisk shaped monument, and Megan could feel him fishing in his trousers with his free hand. "How does that taste, Reggie?" he laughed, emptying his bladder in a zig-zag pattern across the white marble. Megan thought about trying to wiggle free while he was occupied, but the others were right there, sneering at her through black teeth. It was no use. She wouldn't get far.

When he finished relieving himself, he snorted and spit, and then walked further into the heart of the cemetery toward a mausoleum. With a single kick of his giant foot, he opened the door and started down a flight of stone steps.

Choking and spitting filth from her mouth, Megan managed to look up the stairway just as the door slammed shut.

***

Megan hit the ground with a thud, and hands came out of the darkness to unbind her hands and feet.

"You wait here, little one," her captor said.

It was pitch black, damp, and smelled of clay. Something with more than two legs crawled across her hand and she shook it off and hugged her knees and tried to relax. She had been in the land of the dead twice since her suicide attempt, and it was never the same. The only consistent thing about dead people was that they preyed on your fears. Lost souls were annoying, but dead people were ruthless.

"Are you lost?" A raspy female voice emerged from the darkness.

"No," Megan said, "my name is Megan Worthington and I live with my father at 516 Barksdale Lane."

"I don't see your father anywhere, little one. I think you might be lost." Megan could feel the presence getting closer, until it covered her like a shroud in the darkness. The hairs on the back of Megan's neck stood up. "You've been here before, Megan Worthington."

An aura of dull blue light filled the small room where Megan sat. A dead woman crouched in front of her, her ragged gown and ratty white hair covered in dirt. Megan's wrist began to burn, not the white hot touch Joseph had given, but a raw, sharp sting. She could feel the warm, wet flow of her blood begin to drip down her hand.

"Oh, yes," the woman said, "you *have* been here before." She smiled and ran her fingertip across the dark red liquid. Megan clamped down on her wrist, but it only made the blood flow faster. She could feel her life draining away, just like it did that night in her bathroom. The woman licked her bloody finger and smiled. She grabbed Megan's arm and forced her hand away from her wrist. She let out a satisfied moan as she ran her cold, black tongue up Megan's arm, flicking it back and forth across Megan's pulsing scar until the blood slowed and then stopped.

"I'm not lost," Megan said, wrenching her hand free and folding her arms tight against her chest. "My name is Megan Worthington, and I live with my father at 516 Barksdale Lane. I help lost souls get to the other side. I don't belong here."

"You're lost!" the woman shrieked. Her black eyes burned with hatred. "There is no other side. *This* is the other side. You're lost and you're a liar." The woman crawled around Megan on all fours, like a predator surveying its prey. "Lost souls belong to me," she whispered into her ear. "Don't you like me, Megan Worthington?"

"I don't belong here," Megan said calmly.

"Then why are you here?" she mocked. "You wouldn't be here if I didn't own you." She brushed her cheek against Megan's ear and whispered, "I think you miss your mommy."

That comment hit its mark. Megan momentarily lost control of her emotions and lunged at the woman, striking her underneath the chin with the palm of her hand and sending her back on her haunches. Megan's victory only lasted a second.

With fresh fury, the woman roared, grabbed Megan by the shoulders and pinned her to the floor. "Mine!" she growled.

In the next instant, the dirt floor of her prison turned to liquid, and Megan started to sink. She thrashed her arms, struggling to keep her head above the brackish water. Against her will, her arms folded in on themselves, and she sank. The woman watched from the surface of the water as Megan settled on the bottom. She thrashed her legs, searching for a foothold until they became heavy, like two concrete blocks anchoring her to the floor of her liquid prison.

Megan was helpless, her ears ringing, her lungs burning, her mind going numb. She belched out what was left in her lungs, desperately trying to suck air from the water around her. Her mouth twitched, searching for air as the small halo of bubbles floated lazily upward and broke the surface. The menacing face of the dirty, white-haired woman shimmered above. Her blue aura was outlined by a hazy black ring that slowly took Megan's world out of focus and swallowed it whole.

***

23

"Megan." The sweet sound of her mother's voice materialized in the darkness. "Megan, it's me."

For an instant, Megan could feel the cold embrace of the foul depths of her prison, but in the next, she was home, sitting on the swinging bench in her backyard. Megan heard birds chirping, and a soft summer breeze whispered through the trees. Her mother sat next to her, gently rocking the bench with her feet.

"Mom!" Megan reached over and hugged her mom as hard as she could, sobbing into her shoulder.

"Oh, Megan," her mom said. She stopped rocking and ran her fingers through Megan's hair, tucking a few stray wisps behind her ears. "Why are you here, sweetie?"

"It was an accident," Megan said without looking up, "I shouldn't be here. I'm scared mom, where am I?" She searched her mother's eyes.

"Right now, you're trapped between life and death, Megan." Her mother started the bench swinging again.

"What do you mean, like a lost soul?" Megan asked.

"No, not like a lost soul," her mother said, "a lost soul is on its way to the place beyond this world. The souls trapped here can never move on, Megan." She stopped swinging and looked Megan in the eyes. There was love in her eyes, genuine, unconditional love. Megan hugged her mother tighter still. She didn't want to be anywhere else. "Now, I'll ask you again," her mother said. "What are you doing here?"

"I told you, mom, it was an accident – honest," Megan said, burying her face deeper into her mother's auburn hair.

"Megan, the first time you came to find me, I told you we couldn't be together. Do you remember?" her mother asked.

"Yes."

"You have to stop, Megan. It took almost everything I was, and ever will be, to send you back to your father that night."

"But I miss you, mom," Megan said. "Why can't I stay here with you, just like this? We can talk and laugh. I can tell you all about what dad and I have been doing." Megan straightened up. "He's a shift supervisor at the plant mom, you'd be so proud of him! He works so hard to keep our lives together. And I graduated this year. I had to take summer classes to make up for my lost time, but I did it. I did it, mom. Aren't you proud of me?"

"Of course I am, Megan," her mother replied, "I'm proud of both of you. I know all about your lives. I've watched you grow into a confident and capable young woman." She took Megan's hand and kissed her scar. "And I've watched powerless, as you made horrible mistakes, Megan. Decisions that can destroy your soul, and leave you trapped here between worlds." She folded her hands over Megan's, and looked her in the eyes. "Your great-great-grandmother and I are watching out for you, but we can only do so much. You have to help yourself. It's time for you to go."

"You mean Angeline?" Megan asked. "But mom, why did you have to leave? It's not fair!" she started to cry again, anchoring her cheek tightly to her mom's chest.

"I'm sorry, Megan." her mother said. She scanned the skies above their house nervously. "I have to go, Megan, and so do you. You and Joseph have work to do. You have to let me go."

Her mother started to blur as Megan's world slowly went black, her words still ringing in her ears. *Let go.*

***

"Let go, Megan!" Joseph shouted. "Let go!"

Megan opened her eyes with a start. She was in the foul water again, the screams of tortured souls echoing through the water. Joseph was tugging at her arms. "Let go! I'm here to help you!" he shouted again. Megan looked down at her hands, and saw the chains twisted around her wrist that had anchored her in the murky silt. "Come on, Megan. We have to go now!"

She looked up to the surface of the water, where she saw Joseph kneeling, and something clicked. Suddenly her lungs ached, and she realized where she was. She loosened her grip on the chains and they fell away from her wrist. In the next moment, the water pushed up with a rush, sending Megan onto her back with a thud. She and Joseph were back in the cell underneath the cemetery. She rolled over and vomited what was left of the foul liquid in her lungs, coughing and gasping.

Joseph pointed behind her. "Run, Megan, now!"

"What?" Megan said. "Where's my mom?"

"Just go," Joseph said. "Run to the car, and I'll meet you there." He took Megan by the hands. "Trust me."

She turned and looked at where Joseph had pointed. A faint glimmer of light illuminated the stone steps leading to the surface. She stood up, wobbled, and slipped on the muddy floor. Flat on her back, she rolled over and crawled as fast as she could toward the steps. When she got to the steps, she turned around to look at Joseph. He was facing the other way, hunched over defensively.

"I don't understand, Joseph. Aren't you coming with me?"

"Just go!" He yelled without looking back. Megan heard the sound of thundering footsteps, and soon, the walls were shaking around her.

"Hey, where are you going, little one?" The large man that had captured her was running straight at her. Megan watched as Joseph pounced, knocking both of them to the ground. He worked swiftly, attacking the beast in a blur of motion. The man roared in pain, his muddy, writhing body shaking the ground while Megan stood watching.

Terrified, she clamored up the steps on all fours, her muddy shoes slipping and slowing her progress until she burst through the door and fell onto the wet grass outside the mausoleum. The sun was just breaking the horizon, providing enough light for Megan to run the gauntlet of tombstones. She sprinted full speed up over the hill and found the green Taurus right where she parked the night before. She got in and fired the engine.

"Come on, Joseph, where are you?"

"I'm right here," he replied from the passenger seat, "let's go."

Megan hit the gas and sped away. She was soaking wet, muddy, and out of breath. As the cemetery disappeared in her rearview mirror, she finally started to breathe. She turned on the heat and tried to calm down, but when the blast of air hit her legs, the smell of stale urine wafted past her nose. She quickly turned it off and glanced at Joseph, thankful that dead people couldn't smell.

"What just happened, Joseph?" she asked. "How did you do that?"

"Do you understand everything that happens when you help lost souls like me?"

"Of course not."

"Then don't worry about it."

"I don't think so," Megan said. She pulled the car over to the side of the road. "You're not like any lost soul I've ever helped before. You see other dead people in gas stations, you fight off creepers in cemeteries. I know there's something going on here!"

"Look," Joseph said calmly, "dead people can't kill you. You know that. Everything that happens is just in your mind. All I did was help you wake back up to reality, and you did the rest."

"But, how did you know I was trapped in there?"

Joseph sighed, rubbing his eyebrow with his hand. "Your mother reached out to me, and asked me to help you, Megan. She's been talking to me ever since I met you."

"What?" Megan punched Joseph square in the shoulder, as hard as she could. "What the fuck are you talking about? How has she been talking to you?"

"She and I connected, kind of like how you and I do."

"Well, admitting you have a problem is step one, fucker," Megan gripped the steering wheel until her knuckles were white. With an angry grunt, she wound up and punched Joseph in the shoulder so hard the side of his head hit the passenger window. "Can you move on already, and get the fuck out of my life?"

"It's not that simple, Megan, you know that," Joseph said calmly, rubbing the side of his head, "but being at the cemetery did help me."

"What do you mean?" Megan snapped.

"I know what happened in the fog."

"You remember the lighthouse?"

"Yes," Joseph said, "but I can't tell you about it. The words in my head won't come out for some reason. We need to go to the lighthouse, so I can show you."

***

The drive to the lighthouse was quiet. Joseph kept to himself, looking out the window at the water, while Megan's thoughts were heavy with the weight of her mother's death. Seeing her again brought back a flood of emotions. Megan felt like there was a hole in her heart, a small tear in the fabric of her soul. She wanted desperately to help her mother, to go back to when she was seven year's old and somehow change it all, but she knew that was impossible.

The parking lot was barren when they arrived at the lighthouse. It was mid-week and after Labor Day, so the building was only open on weekends. Megan parked the car and downed what was left of the diet soda. Her clothes were nearly dry from her escape in the cemetery, but she was chafing in all the wrong places. She ached for a warm shower and fresh clothes.

She pulled her hair back into a fresh ponytail, and got out of the car. She and Joseph walked over to the rocks where they had first met and Megan sat down on a large, flat boulder. She had spent countless evenings at the water's edge with her dad, watching sunsets and playing in the surf. Some of the best memories she had left of her mother were at the beach. "The lake seems so peaceful," she said.

"It can be," Joseph replied, "but it can also be deadly." He shifted on the rock so he was facing her. "When you're ready, take my hands." This was another first for Megan. Usually, she had to fill lost souls' minds with memories, not be shown them. She took a deep breath and took hold of his outstretched hands.

The images came to her slowly, like Joseph was trying to ease her transition, but soon she was completely lost, deep inside his memories. Joseph stood on the beach, the waves rolling in off the lake in a relaxing, steady rhythm. The lighthouse flickered a counterpoint to the waves, sending its light out into the darkness of the summer night. Angeline was next to him, holding his hand. She smiled, her blue eyes bathed in the moonlight. He brought her hand to his lips and kissed it gently.

"It's like a dream," she said. "You, our life together, it's all like a wonderful dream, Joseph. August can't get here soon enough.

Angeline Foster!" she smiled and spun around with her arms in the air. "I can't wait!"

"I just wish your father-"

"My father is none of your concern," Angeline interrupted. "He'll come around. My father just wants what's best for me. He'll see, Joseph. He'll see what a wonderful, caring and dedicated man you are. Don't worry." She reached up and put her fingers through his hair, brushing it back from his forehead. She smiled, stood up on her tiptoes and kissed him on the cheek.

Just then, Joseph heard a voice across the water. Someone needed his help. He stepped closer to the water's edge and cupped his hands behind his ears. "Help me! My baby, please help me!" a woman shouted from the darkness.

"Joseph, no," Angeline pleaded, "There's nobody there. She's not real!"

"She's there, Angeline," Joseph said, pointing into the black water. "I can see her! She needs my help." He ran past Angeline and down the dock where a rowboat was at the ready. He jumped in, untied its moorings, and started rowing out into the lake.

"Joseph!" Angeline cried from shore, "Joseph, no! Please!"

He ignored her and rowed on toward the sound of the woman's cries. As he got closer, he heard a baby wailing. He rowed harder. "Help us! Please! Please don't leave! Just take my baby! Please!" Joseph stopped rowing and scanned the darkness. A thick fog had rolled in, making it impossible to see the shore. As he rowed on, the faint, rhythmic blur of the lighthouse faded until it too was consumed by the fog. He had to find her. He knew he could save them.

He looked over his shoulder, and there she was, struggling to stay afloat, holding her baby above the water. "Please! Please don't leave us! Just take my baby! Just take my baby!" Joseph stopped rowing and reached out toward the woman and her screaming infant. The white fabric of the woman's dress clung to her body like a shroud, pulling her down. He looked into her panicked eyes, extending the paddle as far as he could. "Here," he cried, "take hold! Don't let go!" but the woman kept floating away, just out of reach. He paddled a few more times and reached his arm out until he was half in the water himself. The woman reached up to hand him her child, but the infant slipped from her grasp into the water. "No!" she screamed, took a breath, and went after her baby. "Don't," Joseph gasped, but it was too late. The woman disappeared into the dark water and never resurfaced.

As Joseph knelt in the boat sobbing, a white handkerchief floated to the surface where the woman and her baby had died. He retrieved it from the water and shouted at the darkness, "Why!" He curled up on his side, rocking with the waves. Slowly the fog cleared, and the lighthouse beacon resumed its silent cadence from shore. The moon that shone down on Joseph's face began to blur as he gently brought Megan back to where they were sitting, on the rocks underneath the lighthouse.

"It's her!" Megan cried in disbelief.

"I know," Joseph said.

"The woman who trapped me in the cemetery – it's her!" Megan started shaking. "Joseph, what's going on?"

"I saved 164 people that night off Evanston. She and her baby were two of the seventy-three souls I lost." He looked down. A tear was cutting a path down his cheek. "She haunted me the rest of my days, Megan. I would hear them on the beach. I would see them struggling in the surf from my watch on the tower. Every day of my life, until –"

"Until you jumped from the tower," Megan finished his sentence.

"No," Joseph said through clenched yellow teeth, "until she pushed me over the edge."

***

Megan looked out over the water. The sun shone brightly against the Caribbean blue of Lake Michigan. It was a stark contrast to the drama she had just witnessed in Joseph's mind. She could tell he was nearly ready. His blank stare had been replaced by a determined, longing expression, and his hazy charcoal eyes were now a lush, crisp green. Against his pale skin and thick black hair, they were mesmerizing. Without thinking, she reached out and took hold of his cold, dead hand. It was stiff and unfeeling, but she felt her heart skip a beat just the same.

"It must have been terrible living with all that guilt," Megan said, "but it shouldn't be long now. You remember your life, you remember how you died. You'll be at peace soon."

"There's something I need to see, Megan," Joseph said without looking away from the water. "My logbook and a few things of mine were hidden in the floor in my quarters. I need to see them before I go."

Megan looked over her shoulder at the lighthouse. They still had the place to themselves. "Alright," she said, "we can see if they are still there." It wasn't the first time Megan had broken into a museum, or ignored a 'please don't touch' sign. There was something about feeling a piece of their own lives that helped lost souls. It was usually the last thing they did before moving on.

She got up from the rocks and walked around to the front entrance. She got onto her back directly in front of the door and shimmied across the porch until her feet were resting next to the doorknob. She coiled her knees toward her head, and gave the door a swift kick with both feet, sending it flying open with a crash on her first attempt. Apparently, the Friends of Shawnee Point Light couldn't afford a deadbolt, let alone an alarm.

Megan got to her feet and walked into the lighthouse. She went past the set of circular stairs leading up the tower, and into the attached house. The front room had a giant candy store display case filled with trinkets and trappings, and an old-fashioned cash register sitting on top. The walls were filled with pictures of the lighthouse, its keeper's, and their families. A small refrigerator stocked with water, juice and soda hummed away in the corner. Megan opened it and grabbed a diet soda.

"So, where am I going, Joseph?" she asked, taking a sip.

"My quarters are on the other side of the kitchen," Joseph replied. He pointed to an open door. Megan could see another room beyond the kitchen, at the end of a neat little runway formed by velvet ropes designed to keep people away from the furniture and assorted maritime knickknacks. Megan walked through the kitchen and stepped over the rope into Joseph's quarters. There was a modest dresser, a bed and a desk against the wall underneath a window facing the lake.

"There," Joseph said, pointing under the desk. "There was a loose board next to the wall. I used to shove it up onto the ledge between the floor and the wall." Megan tapped the floor with her toes, and it rattled in response. She shoved the desk over to expose the board, then pried it up with her fingernails until she could lift it free of the joists. She looked into Joseph's secret hiding place, but saw nothing.

"There's just cobwebs, Joseph," she said. "Somebody must have found it. It's been a long time, you know."

"No, not in plain view," he said. "Reach up under the other board toward the wall. I carved out a ledge just for this. You should find a box."

Megan sighed. She reached up as instructed and found a small opening tucked under the next floorboard. She extended her arm until she was practically up to her shoulder. Her fingertips hit something and it moved. She got her hands around it and brought it out onto the floor next to the desk. It was a small wooden box with a rusted latch. She opened the box and brought out the contents. There was a leather book, something that looked like a dream catcher with a prism suspended from the center, and a mangy white handkerchief.

"Joseph, is this from the accident? Was it hers?" Megan held up the handkerchief. One end was bunched up in a ball and tied up with a piece of string.

Joseph nodded. "I kept in my pocket," he said. "I carried it with me everywhere."

Megan handed the dream catcher and handkerchief to Joseph, and opened the logbook. Nearly 150 years in the floorboards near Lake Michigan had not been kind to the leather, but the pages were mostly legible. The early entries were just as you would expect. There were observations of the weather, the lake conditions at specific times and dates. After about the first month, though, Joseph started adding in other notes and ramblings. *Heard a child wailing down by the beach this morning,* he wrote on one day. *No sleep last night. The woman in white was perched like a spider over my bed,* he wrote on another.

"Joseph," Megan said, "the logbook is full of notes about the woman in the white dress and her baby." She flipped toward the back of the logbook. The pages were filled with crude drawings of the woman and nonsensical ramblings about who she was, and how he had to make her go away.

"I tried to get help," he said, "but most people – even Angeline – didn't believe me. If they did, they didn't know what to do. In my time, asylums were more like prisons than hospitals."

"This journal couldn't have helped," Megan said, fanning the pages. "It makes you look fucking crazy."

She stopped at the final page and looked closer. There was a doodle that looked like a series of connected concentric circles with shafts of light coming out from the center.

"Case and point," Megan said, showing him the page. Joseph's eyes glimmered and he smiled as he touched the drawing.

"It isn't nonsense," he said. "I found a book – a couple books actually – that were pretty helpful. There's a lot of hidden power and energy in those symbols." Joseph sighed. "Then I went to my priest, but he told me I'd be better off seeing the healer that lived up in the hills outside of town. I think he was just patronizing me, but I went anyway."

"On the Indian reservation?"

Joseph nodded.

"The healer told me my guilt was like a bridge, that it was allowing the spirit into our world," Joseph said. "He gave me the dream catcher and told me how to contact it."

"So, what's the handkerchief for?" Megan asked. "It looks like the tissue ghosts I used to make in art class in grade school."

"That's the key," Joseph said. "He did something to it, cast some sort of spell, I guess. He told me confronting the spirit with it would make it go away, but I never had a chance to try." He looked out the window toward the beach, and put his hand on Megan's shoulder. "I need your help. If I don't drive her away, I'll never find peace."

"I don't know," Megan said, remembering her confrontation in the cemetery. "She's powerful, Joseph. Without you, I think I'd still be trapped in that mausoleum."

"And without you, I'd still be completely lost," Joseph said. "Come on." He handed Megan the handkerchief. "I'll draw her out and you drive her away."

Megan put the book on the floor and stood up. By the time she got to her feet, Joseph was gone. Through the window, she could see him frantically carving shapes into the sand beyond the rocks. He stopped and raised his hands up to the sky as a rumble of thunder rattled the window. Off in the distance, she could see dark clouds forming over the lake.

Megan cursed Joseph under her breath, tucked the handkerchief into her pocket, and ran.

***

When Megan got to the beach, the woman in white was there. She stood in the surf about ten feet from shore, her tattered dress clinging to her dirty wet body. Joseph was standing on the beach, next to a pattern of concentric circles just like the one in the book Megan had retrieved for him. The dreamcatcher was stuck in the sand, right in the center.

"Who summoned me?" The woman growled in her raspy voice.

"You're not wanted here!" Megan shouted at the woman. "You can't have Joseph. He doesn't belong to you. He deserves to move on!"

"Don't test me," the woman sneered at Megan. "I take who I want, and Joseph Foster belongs to me." She glared at Joseph and her body changed form. One second she was a large middle-aged man, and the next she was a skinny young girl – a seemingly endless stream of men, women, and children –all with the same desperate look on their faces. "I took many souls that night, didn't I Joseph Foster? But this one seems to suit you the best." She resumed her form as the mother in the white dress.

Megan walked between Joseph and the woman and put her hands out defensively. "You're not taking Joseph. He's moving on, and you're going back where you came from."

In an instant, the woman was in Megan's face, shrieking. She grabbed Megan's throat with an iron grip and squeezed. "I don't know how the two of you escaped, but I'm taking him back." She let go of her throat with a shove. "And I'm taking you, too."

Megan's heart was pounding through her chest. She reached into her pocket and felt the handkerchief, but then hesitated. The wind was blowing harder, and a flash of lightning filled the sky. She glanced back at Joseph for reassurance, but he wasn't there. "Joseph," she called, scanning the beach and the rocks. He was on top of the tower, a black shadow against the darkening skies. "No, Joseph! Don't jump!" Joseph was gripping the guardrail, the white spirit right next to him, shouting in his face.

Without hesitating, Megan started to run. She ran up the path from the beach, in the front door, and started up the steps. Her legs ached and her lungs burned, but she ran on, pulling herself with her arms as she went up the stairs. "Joseph, no!" she screamed as she flung herself onto the observation deck.

The woman's words cut through the howling wind at Joseph. "You couldn't save them, Joseph. You let her baby die, her screaming, innocent little baby. You killed them!"

Joseph clamped his hands over his ears and let out a desperate cry. He dropped to his knees and looked up at the woman through clenched teeth. She stood over Joseph and roared, no longer the white haired woman in the tattered dress, but a twisted, grotesque spirit. The black and gray hues of the spirit's aura emanated out like jagged spears, piercing Joseph's head. He screamed again, scrambled to his feet and grabbed the guardrail.

Megan's mind raced. She couldn't bear the thought of Joseph going back to the land between worlds. He didn't deserve eternal damnation. He deserved to move on. Pulling the handkerchief from her pocket, she gasped as Joseph put his leg up on the rail and coiled his other leg to jump. "No!" Without thinking, Megan thrust the handkerchief into the black cloud surrounding Joseph, and grabbed onto him as tightly as she could.

As the three of them touched, time seemed to stand still, and something stirred deep inside Megan. It wasn't so much a feeling as a connection, a beacon of hope that she only carried for Joseph. She felt it the first day he touched her, and without knowing, had been nurturing it ever since. She let go of the light, gave it to Joseph, and it enveloped them all in a blinding white flash.

***

Megan awoke on the rocks near the beach. She rubbed her neck and temples, and tried in vain to massage away the throbbing ache that had invaded her skull. As she sat up, a familiar silhouette appeared between her and the setting sun. Joseph stood with his hands in his pockets, looked down, and smiled.

"Did it work?" Megan asked.

"I think so," he said. "I don't completely understand where I'm going, but I know she isn't there waiting for me." Joseph held out his hands and helped Megan to her feet. His hands were soft, almost warm, and his face was flushed and full of life. "I didn't want to leave without saying goodbye."

"So, you're ready then?"

Joseph nodded.

"It's about fucking time."

Lost souls rarely said goodbye, but Megan was glad he did. Part of her wanted nothing more than to have Joseph out of her life, but part of her didn't know what she would do without him.

Joseph turned and started to walk down the beach.

"Hey, Joseph!"

As he stopped and turned around to face her, she wound up and threw a rock the size of her fist directly at his head. He raised his arms to protect his face, then disappeared just as the stone reached his forehead. It landed in the sand with a soft thud and rolled into the nearby dune grass.

"You're welcome."

Megan brushed the sand and dirt off the back of her pajama pants and walked up the path toward the car. After she knocked the sand out of her running shoes, she sat down behind the wheel and dug in her purse. She turned on her cell phone and poked the screen with her thumbs.

I'll be home in a little while, she texted her dad.

The Vanishing of Princess Devonswan

Daniel Hunter

The band of soldiers fought their way inside the gates despite massive resistance, barely breaching the vestibule. Victor led the charge as valiantly as possible despite the inner disquiet brought on by the abominations he had already faced, forcing his way down an adjoining hallway. It was then that a portcullis fell behind him, isolating the leader from the rest of his group.

With the gate to his back, he pressed further down the hall, fighting solo against more foes, praying for their swift defeat and a way to rejoin his soldiers.

But the army they stood up against was formidable, and unnatural.

Armored from head to toe, everything from their steel boots to their horned helmets were black as night, aged and a bit rusty perhaps, but Victor could tell they were once of the finest quality. Their clothing was tattered and faded, and dirt stained as if they had just crawled out of the grave. Which explained why they reeked of decay.

The horned soldiers fought fiercely, but they fought silently. Only hollow echoes rang out with each blow of his weapon against their breastplate. There were no cries of pain, no howls of morale, and even more eerie to him was the fact that there were no strenuous grunts as they swung their weapon. They came from somewhere, and someone commanded them to fight. The Master of Wraithfall Castle was no doubt a terrible foe.

After dodging and blocking the swinging swords of the enemy, Victor counterattacked. With one vertical strike his battle-axe sliced through the armor of one of the deadly foe. At last his shield deflected an attack from the last foe, and Victor swung his axe into his legs, crushing his armor and dropping him to the ground. Neither made a sound as they fell to the ground.

He couldn't, *wouldn't,* believe that they were anything other than human despite the evidence gathered by his very senses. He briefly considered raising the visor on one of the horned helmets, just to prove they were human. As nerve-wracking as it may have been to do so, he would have if there were time. Reuniting with his soldiers in combat took priority. Victor ran down the hall, looking for a corridor to reconnect with his men, but there was something disturbing about this castle. He couldn't find a way back to the vestibule where his knights were most likely still fighting. He always believed he had a good sense of direction, but no matter how hard he tried, he couldn't find his way back.

Just when he felt he could walk no further, he came upon a beacon of peace amidst the ruin of decay in which he had been wandering.

Serenity.

At last, it was within his grasp.

As the weary knight from the Order of the Word pushed open the heavy oaken doors, air escaped the abandoned room of worship and washed over him as if it were a living entity, replacing his fear and weariness with a profound sense of peace.

The beauty of the chapel, deserted long ago, was still discernable through thick layers of dust along rickety pews and sacred relics. It remained a sacred bastion within the evil domain. He sighed, tired, wounded and alone. His own blood, and that of his men, stained his white tunic and once-shining silver armor. Without hesitation the knight stepped into the chapel of the aberrant castle and closed the doors behind him, sliding a large walnut bookcase containing the chapel's hymnals against them to serve as a barricade.

Confident that he could take a short moment to rest, he exhaled and murmured quietly, "Praise be to God." The knight turned his attention to the room while dropping to a knee from fatigue.

Fully taking in the chapel, he was awe-inspired by its beauty and innate tranquility. The veteran knight looked up to the cross hanging thirty feet over the pulpit and offered a silent prayer. It was a simple wooden cross, but it was so large that it commanded attention as the focal point of the room. The chapel appeared untouched as if it were preserved and protected with God's very hand, in contrast to the remainder of the castle.

Just outside roamed creatures of unimaginable malevolence. The beings should not, in truth if he had been asked just a day ago would have claimed they *could not,* have existed. Abominations to the world... perhaps even to God. Where was God? Was he perhaps still here, in the mystery of this hidden sanctuary?

His mind wrestled with what he had seen, what no one would have ever believed possible.

Once again he looked upward to the cross. It was not unlike the one he had given to her, to the Princess. Of course, hers was made of silver, hung on a thin chain, and much, much smaller.

But it was still a cross.

Two Years Earlier

"I love it!" she cried as she pulled the silver cross out of the tiny box. Princess Karina Devonswan threw her arms around Sir Victor Winchester, the veteran knight assigned as her personal guard and head of her protection detail.

He was unprepared for her impulsive act of affection, transparent by his hesitation and cautious manner of returning her hug. He didn't think she noticed his pause, but he had to be careful with boundaries of appropriateness.

"Will you put it on me, Victor?" Immediately she handed him the box, expecting and quite certain of a yes despite the way she phrased her question. She pivoted her body away from him and pulled aside her long blond hair, exposing her soft, warm neck to him.

Again he hesitated. He silently cursed under his breath, realizing he acted against his better judgment. He should have given her the gift in the presence of the king and queen.

Countless times he had reminded her to address him as Sir Winchester, as was simple protocol, but lately she'd grown into the bad habit of calling him by his given name. Maybe it was because he was caught off guard, but for the first time he hadn't corrected her.

He told himself she was blameless, reacting with the enthusiasm of a child. Both of her parents trusted him, which is why he was chosen to be her protector in the first place, but she was getting older. Soon enough she would be able to bring him to that uncomfortable point despite the age gap. Had he been younger the situation could have been different, but admittedly also more volatile.

There was also perception. When it came to the royal family, perception was everything. Like it or not it was just a cold, hard reality. Victor knew he needed to convince her to spend more time with her Ladies-in-Waiting.

He grimaced with the realization that it might be time for him to step down and make sure his predecessor was a female knight of the Order of the Word.

Present Time
As his eyes fluttered open, the first thing he saw was the woven tapestry of the Last Supper hanging crookedly on the wall. He sat

upright on the pew, tilting his neck from side to side to work out the kinks. His muscles were still sore from the recent battle, and falling asleep in his armor didn't help.

It was hard to tell how much time had passed; fifteen minutes or fifteen hours, he wasn't sure. No matter. Despite his soreness he still felt rejuvenated. Judging from the lack of sunlight against the stained glass windows he guessed it was still before dawn. Then again, the sun didn't seem capable of penetrating the thick rolling fog surrounding the forlorn kingdom.

Little was known about the castle because until just a few days ago no living creature had ever entered the gates of Wraithfall Castle. Legends handed down through time spoke of a great evil that rested inside. And now here he was, deep inside the walls of the very castle that he had been told as a boy was not only haunted but evil to the core.

Princess Karina's great-great grandfather ordered the highway road closed just before the mountain pass that led up toward Wraithfall Castle, and it remained that way until the present time. The ancient castle sitting high upon the cliffs at the end of the mountain range looked down and into the dark sea below. Throughout the years, whenever the occasional villager turned up missing, a great debate followed. Some believed the unfortunate soul succumbed to the natural elements, perhaps slipping off a cliff or getting eaten by a hungry bear, while others believed they made the mistake of straying too close to the castle, falling victim to a more sinister evil.

A common rite of passage among the local teenagers was daring to venture beyond the old wooden warning sign that blocked off the road just before the pass. Every All Hallows Eve, many youth ventured out to set up a bonfire a mere hundred meters down the pass, but that was the extent of their bravery.

No one within recollection came anywhere near Wraithfall Castle.

That is, until a few days ago, when Princess Karina vanished.

Victor shuddered, recalling the incident with regret. Could he have prevented all this?

"You're being unreasonable, Victor!" she declared.

The eighteen-year-old princess crossed her arms, challenging his authority.

"Your mother and father. Would they actually allow you to attend one of these All Hallows Eve parties? The Royal Princess of Shandwick, drinking and fraternizing with common folk outside of a sanctioned royal event? Does that sound reasonable to you?" he pointed out, thinking she must surely see what she asked was impossible.

"Of course it does," she said without missing a beat. "If you were to ask them. They trust you, and I trust you. You know they would be fine with it. It's not until tomorrow night, so you'll have plenty of time to make sure the area is safe...or whatever it is you do. It will be harmless."

"It's not safe for anyone to cross the King's Highway toward the mountain pass, especially on All Hallows Eve of all nights. Surely you should know this is asking for trouble."

"Well, fine. If that's how you want to be. You know, maybe Damon can watch over me, or someone else can, if you aren't willing to do your job."

"Fine," he said with barely a whisper. "We shall let the king decide."

He pushed himself to his feet and pushed the painful memory away.

Long separated from the other knights of the order, Victor believed he had moved deeper into the castle than his fellow brothers and sisters, but he couldn't be sure.

He knew he would have to journey even further into the heart of the castle.

Alone.

There was always a chance the princess had already been found and escorted safely out of the castle by his fellow soldiers, but he wasn't optimistic. It was possible they had all died or been driven back during the siege.

For now, he had to focus on the original task at hand, finding Princess Devonswan. Wherever she was, she was also alone and had to be scared. Terrified. If she was still somewhere within these castle walls he vowed to find her. He prayed it would be before anything happened to her.

With a new resolve and determination, Victor stood tall, grasped his steel battle-axe and readied his iron shield adorned with a bright crimson cross – the symbol of the Order of the Word – and prepared to leave the tranquility of the sanctuary.

With one last prayer on both knees before stepping out into the dark unknown, he asked God for wisdom, protection, guidance… and most of all, for the safety of the princess.

***

Nothing was as it seemed within the stronghold's walls. The area was vast and disorienting. It was hard to discern his exact location even by looking outside the windows. Most of the hallways and staircases were straight and simple, yet there were some that randomly curved and jaggedly twisted with no pattern or logic. A few hallways led to dead ends. One staircase led straight up at such a sharp angle a ladder would have been more appropriate, while another staircase simply ended in midair. Victor found one door that, when opened, revealed nothing but a stone wall. Yet another doorway stood in the center of a random room, surrounded only by its stone arched doorframe.

More than once he caught the movement of something shadowy out of the corner of his eye, as if dark, sinister claws were surreptitiously reaching out for him. Yet when he turned to engage the threat, the flickering shadow turned out to be nothing more than branches swaying in the wind just outside a window, illuminated by the flash of a sheet of lightning.

Even his ears seemed to play tricks on him. He could have sworn he heard the sound of a lone violin off in the distance, perhaps on the other side of the castle. Hoping he could find the source of the violin, potentially someone with Princess Karina, Victor tried to isolate the location of the haunting melody, but as he moved closer the music abruptly stopped, making him wonder if he actually did hear anything at all or if it was only his imagination.

Shadows flickered from Victor's torchlight, crudely dancing down the long hallway until swallowed up by the darkness, but he pressed forward. Paintings lined the hallway, individual portraits supposedly of former residents of Wraithfall Castle. They were faces from another time, several centuries past.

Victor slowly stepped into the dark corridor, torch in his shield hand and his battle-axe at the ready. It felt as if the eyes of every portrait were gazing upon him. He singled one out and studied it carefully.

The old man in the portrait, dressed in a fine black suit fashionable from ages long ago, had long grey wisps of hair coming out from underneath his top hat. Thick, grey eyebrows sat above a dark and intense stare from his eyes. The slight cracks in the oil canvas made his scowl even more unnerving, and his eyes looked to the left…directly where Victor was standing.

A loud crashing sound in the distance quickly snapped his attention down the hall; it sounded like a metal serving tray had been dropped, or perhaps one of the hollow suits of armor adorning the hallway had tipped over. Victor took a few steps forward and readied himself into a combat stance.

While the source of the noise appeared close at hand, Victor couldn't isolate where the clanging had come from. After staring down the hall, fully alert and unnerved for a full ten minutes Victor was convinced nothing more would happen. He brought his attention back to that of the old man.

Again the old man stared angrily at Victor, which wouldn't have been a problem, except Victor had moved his position, which meant the eyes of the painting were now looking to the right.

The Hallway of Portraits, he decided, held no useful secrets. Victor pressed forward, heading deeper into the castle. It wasn't long afterward that he once again heard the sound of the lone violin. Although the unsettling requiem chilled him to the bone, it was clear what he had to do. Victor quickly raced down a long, dark hallway – much narrower than any hallway he had previously passed through – chasing after the music.

Strangely, as he surged through the darkness it sounded like the lingering melody shifted from far ahead of him to well behind him. Victor, perplexed but determined, quickly backtracked down the hallway and much to his surprise found himself not in a familiar location, but instead in a completely different section of the castle that he had never seen.

Impossible! In spite of sketching a map of the route he traveled in the castle, Victor scratched his head with confusion.

The hallway dumped Victor out onto a mezzanine, perhaps high upon the third level, overlooking one of the Grand Halls of the castle. The great room must have been at least one hundred feet high from the ground level to the vaulted ceiling; several tall, narrow and pointed windows stretched far up toward the high Gothic arches.

The enormous room – which in itself was larger than most mansions he had ever seen – contained at least four open levels that connected with six separate red-carpeted staircases, maybe more from what Victor could tell from his limited viewpoint (given that several stone pillars obstructed his view). Two of the staircases connected the third-level mezzanine he stood on to the next upper and lower levels.

This wasn't at all what Victor was expecting. That hallway he had just come from… he had *already* been down that hallway… and back; he was sure of it. Yet the mezzanine wasn't there before; the hallway previously didn't connect to it, but it did now. It was as if the very walls were alive, shifting and changing rooms when he wasn't looking.

Because he was down to his last torch, which he vowed to save for an emergency, he held the rudimentary map up to a nearby glass window which caught bleak rays of nocturnal illumination from the moonlight. Still, all the light in the world couldn't help him decipher his own map.

And to make matters worse, the music stopped again.

This was maddening! Even if he could find Princess Karina, he wasn't so sure he could find a way out of this place. He'd covered at least thirty different rooms on three different levels, yet it seemed like he was getting nowhere.

But strangely enough he still hadn't encountered any resistance. If he didn't know any better he would have thought that he was all alone in the dark castle. Yet ever so often, he could swear he felt the presence of someone else…or *something* else. Besides, where was the silent, dreadful army he ran into at the castle gates?

With those thoughts swirling in his head, fear gradually returned to him, like an unwanted presence creeping back into his life. It whispered in his ear, reminding him that odds were high that the other knights had been driven back if not slaughtered, and no one was with him to help explore this fortress of evil. But Karina needed him. As unnerved as he was, a seasoned warrior who knew of combat and war, she had to be *terrified*. Wherever she was.

Yea though I walk through the valley of the shadow of death, Victor prayed silently, *I will fear no evil, for Thou art with me…*

The distant sound of a weeping child drifted from somewhere deep within the fortress.

It had been a long time since his ears had heard the gravely distressed cries of a child – not since he was a fledgling knight, newly assigned as Princess Karina's personal protector, back when she was but a little girl.

He stood still to listen, confused. But in this forsaken stronghold, what could a child possibly be doing in a place like this? If he were lucky, maybe Karina would be found with the child.

Clenching his battle-axe he quickly bounded up the stairs. He finally came to a door behind which he suspected the sobbing was coming. To his surprise, the door was already cracked open. Every door he had encountered until now had been closed. Whatever lie behind the door, he would be ready.

Releasing his tight choke on the battle-axe, he carefully lowered his arm and let the shaft slide though his fingertips until the blade nearly touched the floor, grasping the handle again at the base. With his other hand, he carefully pushed open the door.

An old study lie before him, one that potentially could have seemed cozy or warm, but within these walls it instead appeared dark and stoic. Even with the flickering flames dancing within the fireplace, lapping at the firewood as if it were a living, feeding creature, the room still seemed oddly dim. A high-backed chair faced away from Victor and toward a rather long writing desk. Several books cluttered the right side of the desk while on the left, a small jar half-full of ink with two black writing feathers used its meager weight to try and flatten a small stack of yellowed scrolls.

An adjoining doorway within the room was also open, revealing a nursery – as well as the source of the crying.

Maintaining his focus inside the study – he would get to the nursery in a moment – Victor knew there was someone sitting in the chair even though he couldn't see past the chair's tall back. There was an unmistakable presence; for good or ill he couldn't be sure, but he suspected the later as the oppressing force against him that he felt the moment he first entered the castle had amplified as soon as he stepped into the study. Nonetheless whomever sat in the chair would be the first person he encountered since becoming separated from the other knights, and perhaps he or she might have an answer as to the whereabouts of Karina.

Filled with a sense of uneasiness, Victor slowly walked toward the front of the chair. His heart leapt with both astonishment and discomfort – the chair was empty! And just as suddenly, the room no longer felt as if there were two, but only one.

As if that wasn't enough depravity, the crying stopped almost instantly – hauntingly so – not like a normal child turning his fits of sobbing into a few whimpers before winding down and falling asleep. It was deathly abrupt. And then all became quiet. Only the crackling of the fire reminded Victor he hadn't gone deaf.

Uncertain if his senses were betraying his body, Victor began to doubt his own instincts, the same instincts that made him the knight that he was today. He quickly rushed to the next room, hoping for some sign of the crying child. The crib was empty and every possible hiding place in the room was vacant of all but centuries of cobwebs and dust.

All that was left for Victor to discover was a deep sense of frustration. This place was playing with his mind – driving him absolutely mad. Exasperated, he returned to the study. He was about to leave when he took one last look at the fireplace and hesitated. Why was the fireplace lit? What need would there be to keep warm if the castle was supposedly uninhabited, save for the abnormal mysterious army at the castle gates (and that was assuming they were of the living)?

Victor returned to the desk with the books and scrolls. A thin layer of dust covered the surface, proving that living hands had not been in contact with the desk in quite some time. Yet as he carefully tilted the ink jar, the liquid flowed gently revealing it was far from dried up. Carefully he lifted one of the feathered pens a few inches above the jar; droplets of ink trickled back down into the black solution before he set it back down.

Even stranger was the fact that the books were dusty but the scrolls were not. Victor moved the jar of ink and carefully sorted through the parchments; he didn't stop to count how many. The top scroll was blank but still he quickly flipped through the loose pages. About halfway through he saw writing; each and every page after that, completely filled from top to bottom, had some sort of script.

A chill ran down his spine as he took in the psychotic repetitive scribbling. It read: "Thou shall not kill thou shall not kill thou shall not kill…" over and over until it filled up the parchment completely. The next page contained the same writing, as did the next. In fact, every page with writing had those same four words displayed in a seemingly never-ending cycle.

Then there were the three books. He didn't dare touch them, but he did take note of the titles: *Memento Morieris, The Unforgivable Sin*, and *Where the Styx Ends*. They were unfamiliar titles. But it was obvious death and demise were at their core, and they would do little to serve him in finding the princess.

Just as he turned to leave from the ominous room, he noticed a twinkle out of the corner of his eye. The warm glow from the fire briefly reflected off a silver key sitting on the floor by the corner of the desk. It must have fallen off at one point in time. Carefully he reached down to pick it up, half expecting a trap of some kind, but nothing happened. Flipping the key over in the palm of his hand, he saw a small inscription on the key's head, signifying it belonged to the bedchambers of royalty. It reminded him of Karina and the moment he discovered she was missing.

It was recent, and on All Hallows Eve. He closed his fingers over the silver key before placing it safely inside one of his pouches.

He wanted nothing more to do with this room of ill-omen. It was time to move on.

Three Days Earlier – On All Hallows Eve, the Night of Princess Karina's Disappearance

The moment he entered her bedchamber he realized she was gone.

He was furious, realizing she had slipped out right under his nose. He wasn't sure if he was angrier with Karina or himself for letting it happen. He took pride in developing as an experienced knight over the years, but it seemed the princess had gained her own degree of shrewdness.

Even her Ladies-in-Waiting didn't know where the princess had gone, though that didn't surprise Victor, given the circumstances.

It was bad enough the king and queen had rejected his request to withdraw from personal security detail not even a full day prior, despite his claim that it was a mutual decision between himself and the princess. Even after reminding the royals that she was technically an adult, Victor was told by the king in no uncertain terms that it wasn't an option and that the two of them best fix whatever problem had manifested between them. And with a, "Yes, your highness," that was the end of discussion. He was to remain her protection guardian, whether either of them liked it or not.

The one advantage Victor had was that he already knew where she would be. Unfortunately, once he and his men arrived, with all of the costumed youth in the area she could have been within ten feet of him and he never would have recognized her.

"Lost in a sea of faces, it would seem, sir," his sergeant calmly noted.

There wasn't a finer sergeant than Colin Aldergrove, even if Colin took an occasional liberty to harass his superior—always in a most respectful way of course. He was capable of making hard decisions during the stress of battle, proved himself always faithful to the crown, and most of all he remained steadfast to the knight's orders, which made Victor's job easier.

"So it would seem," the knight confessed. The bonfire party was not only larger than it ever had been, but unlike the previous years, many of the youth had split off into the mountains and forest, well beyond the normal boundaries.

And of course to make things worse, every costume – from goblins to witches, to court jesters and princesses, and even an occasional fairy or other whimsical creature of fantasy – had some kind of mask.

The sergeant most likely already knew what his commander was thinking, but prompted him nonetheless. "Orders, sir?"

Without breaking his attention away from the crowd, he responded, "I don't care if we have to search them, one by one. I'm a breath away from having them all arrested and rounded up. None of them – or us – should be on this side of the great king's highway closure. Unfortunately I do not know her costume, but it will likely be of a very expensive quality so use that as a measurement. She will likely be with her male friend. Possibly one or two other females, but I expect no more than that. She wouldn't be willing to risk a large number of people knowing her exact location. We must act quickly."

For a moment he thought he saw her. A girl dressed as an angel passed no more than two feet in front of him, although there was nothing angelic about the length of her dress. He couldn't make out her facial features thanks to her sparkling white mask, but the ringlets of her blonde hair looked much like the princess's. He quickly stepped forward and grabbed her arm, startling her.

The frightened angel resisted until she realized a Knight of the Word, not a costumed party-goer, had taken hold of her.

Victor looked at her intently. Within only seconds, his face softened and he let go of her arm, allowing her to stumble away.

The sergeant asked, "Not her?"

Victor shook his head.

"How could you tell?"

"Her eyes. Mask or no mask, I can tell by her eyes."

The sergeant chuckled. "You could tell in less than a second, just by her eyes?"

Victor turned toward Sergeant Aldergrove and gave him a stern look of caution. "Of course. I've been with her since she was a toddler. As long as I've been assigned to her, I can tell you what every inch of-" He flinched, stopping himself in mid-sentence. His stern look vanished, replaced with resign.

He couldn't deny the fact that her crystalline blue eyes sparkled like nothing he had ever seen. She was truly blessed with the wide, beautiful eyes of an angel.

"So should I tell the men they will be able to find her by her eyes?" The sergeant maintained a neutral face, but Victor knew better.

"Get going," Victor commanded, shaking his head, refusing to give any hint of a smile until the sergeant departed.

Continuing to scan the crowd, Victor exhaled. "Where are you, Karina?"

"I think we should head back," Princess Karina warily whispered to Damon, shifting her gaze from the left to the right and back again. All evening guilt had been eating away at her despite her best efforts to push it down and enjoy the night. But straying into the forest, further away from the bonfire, put her on edge. She knew this was all a mistake.

The moon was eerily bright tonight – full and big – but at least it shed light on the forest floor. They had been following the river's edge for the last quarter-mile, the sound of the rapids drowning out all noise from back at the bonfire. Damon had promised to show her something exciting. She didn't want to lose her nerve in front of him, but every instinct told her straying so far from the others was a bad idea.

"Oh, come on," Damon coaxed with an exasperated sigh, removing his pirate captain's hat. "First you ask me to get you out of the castle, and now you want to go back."

"I didn't say I wanted to go back to the castle, just back to the bonfire. We are *way* outside my father's boundaries."

"You'll be fine. No one knows we are out here. You'll be back before you know it. I thought you wanted to live a little? Was your sense of adventure nothing more than talk?"

"Fine," she snapped, "but it better not be much further. Whatever is it that is so important you want to show me? And you better not try anything!"

Damon smirked, yet wisely remained silent.

That wasn't a good sign. Karina was not having fun. She was carrying her high heels because they kept getting stuck in the soft soil of the forest floor. Not only were her feet becoming sore, but she had ruined her favorite black stockings. The last thing she needed was for Damon to put the moves on her. She thought he was okay, before tonight, before this stupid stunt he was pulling, but now she was getting annoyed.

She adjusted her French maid's dress, pulling it down and straightening her small lacy apron. If Victor could see her now, he would tell her to stop fidgeting.

Actually, if Victor could see her now, he would probably become enraged.

She must have chuckled out loud because Damon asked, "What's so funny?"

The thought of Victor's reaction brought a smile to her face. In fact, she could have sworn she heard him calling her name.

"Karina! Princess Karina!"

Her eyes widened. He *was* calling her name. He was yelling so loudly, she could hear him from across the river. The princess gasped with disbelief, astonished that he had found her this quickly. Somehow he *knew* it was her, despite the gold-lined black masquerade ball mask across her face. It should have been at *least* a few more hours before he discovered she'd left the castle!

She scoffed as Damon bolted, that coward. Of course Victor did have a longbow in his hand and looked angry enough to use it. He was a sweetheart. He'd never use it anywhere near her. Well, maybe Damon didn't know that.

She planted her hands on her hips. Even though she knew she was in trouble her stubborn nature refused to give Victor any leniency. "What are you doing here? Go! You're not welcome," she shouted angrily across the river.

Victor looked up and down the river, and then took a step forward. Her heart skipped a beat. It looked as if he was actually considering plunging into the icy cold water, risking certain death against the rapids, just to take her back under his control.

"Are you insane? Don't you even *think* of it, Victor! You'll drown!" she shouted at the top of her lungs.

"Listen to me very carefully," he yelled back, holding off for the moment. "Your father will hang *both* of us if you keep avoiding me." Taking a deep breath, Victor shrugged his shoulders and she could imagine him trying to calm himself. "I'm… I'm sorry. I regret our argument," Victor added, removing the arrow from the bowstring.

She could feel her heart softening again. The princess almost cursed her weakness. She wanted to remain upset with him, but it was so difficult to do so. "You wanted to leave me. You wanted another knight to be my guardian."

"We both went down the wrong path."

She smiled.

"You've always been the closest thing I have to a daughter."

She flinched. Daughter? Is *that* what he'd thought of her? She didn't know whether to yell at him for his stupidity, or cry from a broken heart.

Of course he didn't know how she really felt about him… but still.

So maybe it was a crazy childish crush. At first, anyway. It was more than that now. Karina would never forget the time she first began to see him in a different light, no longer simply a handsome knight in her eyes, but a compassionate, caring man. It started back when she was having a really, really bad day. Her beloved dog had just died. She had an awful fight with one of her friends. And of course her studies were particularly difficult that day, for how could she concentrate?

It was Victor who identified her struggle and sat down next to her, simply offering to help with her schoolwork. Her friends, Ladies-in-Waiting, and even her parents, none of them seemed to notice the heartache she was going through. Of course she put on a brave front that fooled everyone else, everyone except Victor.

And here he was again, always showing up and protecting her. She knew it was his job, but she couldn't help but wonder if he thought of it as more than just that? Having softened a little, she asked him, "How did you find me anyway?"

"We found some drunks that recognized what's-his-mask, your semi-noble pirate friend who bravely ran away," he said, with a touch of disdain. "They saw you two sneaking off this way."

Placing her hands behind her back and pursing her lips, she looked away, eyes downcast. Just the word sneaking made her feel remorseful. Suddenly her eyes opened wide. After a brief moment the intent of his words had hit her, and she was mortified! He must have thought the worst about her. No wonder he had been furious up until this point! This was about more than sneaking off, she reasoned.

Quickly she blurted, "It's not what you think!" Now she was seriously worried. If this got back to her father and mother, they would tar and feather her. But even worse than that was Victor's perception of her.

"But of course. And in return, I shall show *him* something," Victor said, subtly brandishing the tip of his arrow that reflected the moonlight off of the sharp, cold steel.

As they had been speaking, he'd been walking further upstream, where the river widened from a narrow torrent and the white water slowed to a quieter stream making a crossing possible.

She gasped, "You wouldn't!" Yet to her surprise, she found herself admitting, in a twisted sort of way, that it was incredibly romantic. Butterflies tickled her stomach.

"Oh, I would." But he actually laughed, "Relax. I do believe you, Princess Karina, if that is what you are sincerely telling me. But him, I do not trust. You *must* be more careful."

With a deep sigh of relief, the princess realized that he trusted her. She had her moments of defiance, and this latest was a big one, but she never had lied to him.

By the way, I love the irony," he added.

She hurried along the riverbank to keep up with him and looked back at Victor, somewhat puzzled. "What?"

"I imagine tonight a fair number of maids have dressed up as princesses, yet you chose to do it quite contrary. A princess, dressing as a maid."

She could tell he was smiling with amusement simply by the way he pronounced his words. No one else could have detected the subtle nuances of his speech, but she knew him better than anyone else.

"Even in an outfit as risqué as that. Still, I have always known your lifelong desire to see how life marches on through the ordinary, mundane life, far outside of your royal lineage. So I do understand the satire."

"So you've seen my outfit," she said with a blush, suddenly feeling close to naked. "But where is *your* outfit, good Sir Knight? It *is* All Hallows Eve after all."

She could have sworn he was smiling as he said, "I'm wearing it. Tonight I am a Knight of the Word."

The princess scoffed, "So boring. You're no fun! You always are a knight. Be rebellious! Try to do something different! Or *be* someone different!"

She heard his deliberate laugh, "Like what, a pirate?" She crossed her arms and huffed. Not only was he making fun of Damon, but he wasn't being any fun, period.

Changing subjects, apparently wanting to get to the heart of the matter, Victor told her, "As far as you leaving the castle, perhaps we can compromise in the future. I am willing to work on becoming less rigid, if you are willing to accept certain limitations?"

She beamed, "I'd like that."

"Me too. But you truly have flirted with danger tonight, and sneaking away without my notice is unacceptable."

His lecture stung, suddenly making her feel half her age. Maybe it was because she had acted half of her age.

He continued, "We will both have to explain this to your father and mother. There is a realistic chance I will be removed from duty, as I am sure you've considered. So our reconciliation may be for naught."

Her eyes widened and she gasped. "No!" She had not considered that her defiance might cause the removal of Victor from his position. Remorse weighed on her heavily, now aware of the fact that her rebelliousness may have potentially caused not only the termination of the brave knight from his duty, but also his removal from her life. The notion was unbearable.

"I do not believe I can save you from this consequence, but perhaps we can lessen the damage. Now please, will you come? Some good has chanced upon us this night. A bridge. Do you see it? The bridge isn't that far. I will meet you there."

"I see it," she said, reluctant to end her moonlight escapade now that it was time to face the music. The first thing she would do when she returned to the castle was beg her parents for forgiveness in hopes that they would refrain from reassigning Victor.

Princess Karina couldn't tell if he could see her smile in the moonlight, given the distance of separation between the two. So what if he thought she was "like a daughter"? She'd make him change his mind.

She reached the bridge, and saw Victor, already halfway across from his side. She raised her hand to wave and he returned the gesture when suddenly an expression of horror descended upon his face.

"Karina, behind you!" he yelled. In one swift motion he had his arrow nocked and pointed in her direction.

She spun around, just as something inky and black webbed out from the deeper shadows of the tree line behind Karina and snared her. Screaming, she struggled frantically, attempting to free herself from the cold, steely fingers that held her arms pinioned to her sides. The way it moved was unnatural. It flickered as it moved like an electrical current, but it was so opaque even the darkness around it dimmed in contrast.

Beating at the air with her fists did little good, but it didn't matter because suddenly something grabbed her wrists, too, and then her waist was encircled by what felt like chill threads that wrapped around and around, but almost instantly, until they became cords of unyielding metallic strength. And they fit themselves securely to their positioning because they were flexible until they stopped moving of their own accord, as if this shadowy being consisted of abnormally long, dark fingers, or mechanical-like tentacles.

Victor, wide-eyed and aiming his bow for something to shoot at, could have sworn he saw two small red orbs within the swirling shadow that rushed around her. They almost looked like eyes. Within mere seconds she was enveloped, and the last thing he saw of her was the frightened look on her face before the darkness swallowed her. And then, whatever it was, it pulled her back into the trees to be swallowed by the forest.

And just like that, assuming she was still alive, Princess Karina was gone. Taken.

She had vanished into the night.

Present Time

The moment Karina was grabbed and pulled into the blackness remained seared into his mind. Every time he closed his eyes he saw her being ripped away, just out of his grasp, and also from his very life. The terror she must be feeling right now. He didn't want to think about it, but it was a difficult thought to block out.

The only thing that caused him to temporarily push that thought out of his mind was the familiar sound of the lone violin, once again echoing throughout the castle.

Victor immediately began to follow the noise, chasing down hallway after hallway, following its twists and turns. Twice he went up a set of stairs and once he went down. He no longer knew which floor he was on.

The music was getting louder and louder, which meant he was getting close. With any luck, he would find whoever was playing the tragic requiem and force them to reveal Karina's whereabouts within the massive castle.

He was almost there. He had to be within one hundred feet of the source. Quickly, Victor turned the corner.

The music stopped.

In front of him and only ten feet down the hallway was a rich oaken door ornately designed with intricate etchings along its age-darkened frame. The elaborate detail and expensive material designated royal inhabitants.

Taking note of the fact that the music died, he soon discovered that the only sound remaining was the murmur of his pulsating heart, rapidly beating inside his chest.

He pulled out the silver key and looked at it in the palm of his hand. The music led him to this door, and he wondered if the key would grant him access. If so, could he assume there were invisible eyes upon him, studying his every move?

But for what purpose?

Carefully he inserted the key and turned it. A soft click alerted him when the key released the lock's tumblers. Now he was almost certain that he was being manipulated, but to what end he couldn't be sure. Maybe the castle itself was alive, watching and waiting. Maybe it would never let him leave.

Pushing those hope-crushing thoughts out of his mind, he once again brought his focus to the task at hand. To the only thing that mattered – finding Karina.

Victor carefully opened the door.

At first, he wasn't sure if the room was a bedchamber of a daughter of royalty, or perhaps the bower of the Lady of the castle, but it was definitely of the highest class once upon a time.

The design of the room was indicative to that of his own princess, with a few notable exceptions. The first of which was the dreary, somber appearance of the room. The flash from another lightning bolt lit up a small portion of the chamber in a dark sea green, perhaps the same shade a metallic statue might become after centuries of exposure to rain, wind, and other harsher elements.

Outside of that deathly green shade, the room was dominated by black – the remaining shadows so well hidden that even the lightning's momentary flash of light couldn't reach them.

But all attention was drawn to the center of the room.

Victor shuddered. Every hair upon his body stood up as he witnessed a body hanging from the chandelier. The unfortunate soul wore a white wedding dress and gently swayed to music only they could hear, suspended by the neck. As the night sky flashed again, the room filled with green and black but this time he could see a white porcelain mask with hollow black eyes upon her face. With a mixture of dread and sorrow, and perhaps a bit of shock, Victor stood transfixed at the sight of the Lady in White.

While the unknown woman was not dressed in the maid's outfit Karina was last seen in, Victor feared this could possibly be her. Carefully he approached, reaching his hand out toward the mask, attempting to overcome the slight tremor in his fingers. Holding his breath in terrible anticipation, he peeled the mask off slowly.

He beheld there was no face. No eyes, no mouth, not even a nose.

A dummy.

It was nothing more than a dressed up mannequin. In a fit of rage, Victor swung his axe as lightning crashed in the background. The rope was severed and the body fell to the floor, landing twisted with its arms and legs sharply bent in an unnatural, deformed position.

Clutching his head, Victor tried to shake off the overwhelming emotions threatening to overtake his body and dissolve his spirit. It felt like he was losing his mind. He hadn't seen a living, breathing creature in as long as he could remember. He began to doubt Karina was even in the castle anymore.

He was tempted to give in to the surging anger controlling his body, desiring nothing more than destroying everything in the room. Victor first turned toward the vanity desk, preparing to strike his own reflection in the mirror and watch the shower of glass shards erupt. But then, through the reflection in the mirror, something caught his eye amidst the jewelry on the desk.

It was a silver cross necklace. The shape of the necklace alone was enough to re-center him, but it wasn't just any cross necklace. It was the same one he gave Karina for her sixteenth birthday. It was given to her not just as a flamboyant decoration, but as a reminder of the hope Christ bestowed all upon dying on the cross.

Carefully he picked it up by the thin chain and allowed the cross to settle in the palm of his hand. He took one big breath and exhaled, thanking the Lord yet again for a renewed sense of faith and sanity.

She was still here in the castle, and he knew he was on the right track, getting closer. He would find her, or die trying.

Every great castle has an archive or library, and Victor knew that would be his best chance to gather information. Surprisingly, the easy part was finding the Grand Library. After he pushed the library doors closed behind him he turned toward the center of the room, he looked up with sheer awe, beholding the largest library he had ever laid eyes on. It was at least twice the size of his king and queen's royal library, perhaps even larger as he had yet to fully explore the majestic and splendid institution. The walls reached up at least eighty feet high, covered wall to wall in books, maps, and archived tomes. It consisted of four floors, maybe even more, as he did not have a full field of vision of the entire library. As it stretched toward the ceiling, it gradually sloped upward until reaching a shallow glass dome forming a central apex.

Yet as vast and splendorous as it was, the archaic nature of the library such as how the dusty bookshelves formed long aisles making up passageways of utter darkness, or how the numerous alcoves were dimly lit, gave it a foreboding appearance.

Dark tattered curtains covered the windows haphazardly, once luxurious but now having given in to the decay of time. An old world terrestrial globe sat quietly upon its wooden stand. It almost looked as if there was just the slightest rotation out of the corner of Victor's eye, but when he looked directly at it, he was certain the navigator's globe remained stationary.

Marble busts of long forgotten men, most of whom scowled back ominously, graced the occasional small niche between bookshelves. As Victor began exploring the library, he took note of the marble strangers, uncertain that they were not looking directly at him. With his shield arm, he took out Karina's silver cross and simply held it, running his fingers over it carefully as if reminding himself he wasn't alone.

After carefully exploring the library, navigating the massive labyrinth of literature for what seemed like hours upon hours, Victor finally found something intriguing in one of the far off alcoves.

There wasn't anything specific that separated this particular nook from any of the others. It was just as dark. Spider webs hung from the corners like everywhere else, and the furniture arrangement was similar. It was a little harder to find, though. He stumbled upon it accidentally after becoming temporarily lost, guided down one of the dark aisles until it emptied out into this small half-octagon area.

Two maroon leather wingback chairs sprawled out from across a small rosewood table adorned with a bronze candelabrum in the center.   A black leather-bound book sat angled and open as if recently read; its matching bookmark rested in the crease.

Victor stepped forward prudently to analyze the book and its text

"...He came on All Hallows Eve, that Stranger. He came from roaming to and fro across the land, seeking an audience with my father, the King. Along the narrow bridge this night and toward the castle's iron gates he trudged along slowly as if invisible chains burdened his shoulders, yet in spite of his old bones, his fingers were more than able to play an eerie tune on his violin. Despite the long walk that may burden one as old as he, his long, gaunt and pale face seemed to secretly convey a sinister and twisted smile underneath his tattered hood.

Notwithstanding his repugnant stature, there seemed to be some kind of a hidden power manifesting underneath his cloak, evident in the way he hauntingly played his violin. The silver moon – that night much bigger than I had ever seen it – seemed to follow him as if also captured by the distorted requiem.

It became colder as he began to speak, as if the Southern winter's air had suddenly arrived, "You have been expecting me, though you may not know it. You have called me, though you do not remember. I am your answer."

The King was entranced, perhaps able to feel the very power bleeding out of the awful pale Stranger.

As if looking into the King's very soul, the Stranger brought forth a black parchment scroll, flicking it open; it unraveled to the floor. "Power I offer you and your line; power of youth, wealth, and even immortality. Power!" The word rolled off of the Tempter's forked tongue with ease, as if his very words held promise. We were all transfixed; almost hypnotized I would say, if

I did not know better. We knew he had power; seductive and sinister he may have been yet the promise of might overwhelmed. And all of this in spite of a warning in the back of my mind. He spoke again, "You need only sign this scroll in red, and our Pact will be complete."

Transfixed to the Tempter, the wide-eyed King shouted, "Yes! Tell me more!" He stood up from his throne, marching down with zeal, fully prepared to sign the Pact. But before the King could reach the scroll, the Tempter quickly pulled it away.

"Skin for skin! Nothing is free, yet my price is fair. I merely ask that you allow me to roam within your castle walls as long as your family line remains on the throne; this is all I ask. What does the wise King say to this? Will he accept my offer?"

And with a resounding "Yes," the King took the black writing quill and, with red ink, signed our royal family into the Pact. Lightning crashed and thunder shook the foundation the moment it had been done, precisely eight minutes past the third hour; our fate was sealed.

A smile from the pale man brought a shiver to my body; never in my life had I been so disturbed from a mere look – let alone a smile – but there was something wicked about it.

Just then, the wind began to blow inside the Great Hall as if a gale of tremendous strength ignored the stone walls much like the wind might ignore a portcullis. The smell of sulfur hung in the air. The torches flickered and the candles went out, and just like that the Stranger – the Tempter – had vanished before our very eyes. Not some trick of a master magician, but a feat of real sorcery. Never had I believed... until that moment. Yet there was an uneasiness that resided within me, second-guessing the decision of the King.

But it was too late. Just like that, on that fateful All Hallows Eve, the Pact was made between The Stranger and The King.

Immortality, as promised, we were given.

But at a horrible price."

Victor sat in the chair, captivated by the story. He wondered if the story were nothing more than a fictional tale, or if it was supposedly a true story? He pitied the author despite the tragic and despiteful actions his father and family had taken. Victor couldn't help but wonder what was on the black scroll – what the Pact consisted of? As the chapter had come to an end, he turned the page to see how the story might continue.

Though we never saw the Stranger again, we knew he wandered the castle halls, just as he said he would. And the Pact was upheld, though it was at a terrible cost.

At first, the riches came quick, power fell into our laps, and a rejuvenated youth befell the entire royal family. Euphoria overflowed inside and around us; it was as if everything we touched turned into gold.

But the ecstasy was not to last. Slowly we began to waste away from the inside out. We still had our wealth, but the joy of it all began to fade away. Our youth remained evident by our skin, but inside, we felt ten times as old. And with that feeling, we strived to gain more wealth because what we had wasn't enough, and suddenly we no longer believed we were as young as we should have been. It wasn't enough. The more we acquired, the less fulfilled we became.

My father, along with all of my brothers and sisters, never seemed to notice this. Only my youngest brother and I. But by the time he and I discovered our very souls were rotting inside and spreading rapidly like a disease, there was nothing we could do.

I watched helplessly as my sisters attempted to beautify themselves further, yet I could tell that they – like I – were becoming more and more hollow the harder and harder they tried. Once the best of friends, they soon became resentful of each other, stopping at nothing to become the fairest... even if it meant sabotaging their own flesh and blood. One sister set fire to my older sister's hair. Yet another sister who wanted to be the most beautiful across the land tried to cut the nose off her very twin.

My brothers, all having benefited from the power of the Pact, continually tried to outdo each other until playful rivalry had turned into a power-hungry, bloodthirsty and disdainful enmity that cost two of them their lives.

I hope they find the peace they seek as they lay still in our graveyard in the ward; hopefully they have found eternal rest within the royal family mausoleum.

But I doubt it.

As for my father: I shall not begin to speak of the atrocities he committed.

Now for my confession. Not of my sins – for they are so grave that I cannot fathom being forgiven – but confession over my writings.

I am ashamed to say not everything in the last chapter was true. No; it was *true, I suppose, but I left something out.*

The Stranger did ask for an invitation into our castle; that much is true. But he also requested something more. A sort of payment was required every seven years... but of what I cannot bear to discuss or admit to. The very notion is the blackest of sins, vile and beyond unforgiveable. Our hearts have been hardened, and our very thoughts have become a dark swirl of shadows. I believe some of my siblings have embraced the darkness while others of us can foresee our own demise, destined to crumble under the weight of this curse… this terrible secret.

That secret shall be taken to my grave.

When I walk up and down the castle halls, my mind is filled with shadows. When I close my eyes to escape them, the shadows still taunt me. As I write this very piece of literature, I can feel them stirring my brain like a kettle of boiling liquid, waiting for it to boil over until I remain hollow.

Peace evades me… in fact I often forget the very meaning of that word. "Peace." I long for it; I do not remember what it feels like anymore, but I know that peace does not share this wretched feeling… like I am feeling now.

If only I could, I would tell that repugnant, pale Stranger to take his power back. Take his riches back. Beg my father to refrain from signing the Pact.

Or, at the very least, let us fade away and die quietly, one by one; let our family line end before our children bear our curse.

Forgiveness… that word echoes hallow and its meaning shrivels in my mind. Can we be forgiven? Can I be forgiven? Impossible!

WHAT HAVE WE DONE?

Victor lamented for the author, pitying at how horrified he must have felt as he slipped into the darkness, believing hope had evaded him. The short story weighed heavily upon his mind, yet it also revealed a small insight into the days gone past of Wraithfall Castle.

As one chapter came to an end, Victor flipped the page to begin another. With furrowed eyebrows and a great sense of bewilderment, he tried to make sense of the remainder of the book. It was all gibberish and nonsense, as if written by a madman. But

Victor could still sense the common theme of a deep remorse and sheer horror.

Flipping the page back and forth, comparing the handwriting, Victor came to the conclusion it was in fact the same author but somewhere along the way his ability to comprehend the normal had been seriously degraded.

Excluding the mad ramblings and undecipherable scribbling, Victor found the story in the previous chapter incredibly intriguing, pondering its meaning after carefully closing the book and wondering about the great tragedy that befell the kingdom. He believed he had learned a little more about the history of the castle but unfortunately it did not help him with Karina.

Maybe if he could dig a little deeper into the roots of the castle, somehow understanding how this place became a bastion of evil, it might help him discover why she was taken and – hopefully – bring to light her whereabouts.

As Victor studied the manuscript of the unknown author in hopes of gleaning insight from the text, a familiar tune penetrated the still and quiet of the dark library.

It was the violin.

He wasn't sure why, but there was something inside him, almost like an innate sense warning him that there was much more to this haunting melody – something he didn't pick up on the last time he heard the music. Almost as if the very music were evil, subtly working its way into his mind, threatening to corrupt and destroy.

It was harder – much harder – to follow the malevolent song given the utter darkness relentlessly attempting to penetrate his heart.

Once again he placed his hand upon the cross necklace, reminding himself of both his service to the Lord and his mission dedicated to finding Karina.

Victor marched out of the library, once more following the ominous music.

Thick cold fog trickled inside the moment Victor threw open the double doors leading to the outer courtyard, slowly rolling inside past his feet and across the red carpet.

He was certain the music came from behind the door, but the moment he opened them the only sound to be heard was that of the wind whistling between the leafless branches.

The fog inside the ward obscured the walls of the courtyard, but from his view the courtyard looked like any other outdoor cemetery. He had to remind himself it was still technically part of the castle. Even the trees were large. Their bark, seemingly black under the night sky, gave an imposing, shadowy presence as they loomed over him. The headstones nearby were old and faded – some cracked and broken – and many were so weathered they couldn't be read.

Off in the distance Victor could hear the repetitive sound of a shovel digging and tossing dirt, repeating the cycle over and over – digging and tossing, digging and tossing – in a slow but steady manner. He hoped to locate the source of the sound expeditiously, electing to step deeper into the misty ward, careful with each step as to avoid tripping over the smaller unmarked gravestones.

Up ahead he could barely make out the slightest hint of yellow light. A small opening in the fog revealed the source of light to be coming from a lit lantern peacefully sitting upon a headstone.

In the lantern's light Victor could vaguely make out the form of a hunchbacked man in a tattered brown cloak, his back toward him, digging up and throwing dirt on top of a nearby pile.

Victor stepped forward ready to finally speak with a living human being – friend or foe, he couldn't be sure – in hopes of getting answers. He remained cautious and alert, wrapping his fingers one by one around the hilt of his battle-axe, ready to draw his weapon if necessary. An old hunchbacked man shouldn't be a threat, but with the constant deception Wraithfall Castle offered, one could never be too careful.

But just as quickly as the fog had parted, it swiftly filled back in, masking the entire scene except for a small trace of the dingy yellow light which strained futilely, unable to peek through. Victor quickly moved forward, but by the time he arrived at the grave the old hunchback was nowhere to be seen. The lantern remained atop the headstone, leaning slightly over the open grave, and the rusty shovel lay unattended on the ground.

Wherever he may have vanished to, assuming Victor could believe his own eyes, was a mystery. He never heard footsteps, but it was possible he ran off into the fog. Then again, it was possible he was nothing more than a hallucination – a figment of his mind. The castle walls tested his sanity more and more with each second he remained within them. Now that Victor stood by the gravesite he noticed something he hadn't seen earlier – an old, shadowy coffin of the darkest ebony wood sitting behind the pile of dirt, silently waiting to be lowered into the depthless void. Ready, yet waiting as if it could wait for an eternity.

Victor grabbed the shovel dand, after walking around the grave, he jammed the shovel's tip between the coffin and the lid and pried it open.

And inside, he discovered a body.

Maggots crawled over the body inside the coffin, infesting the deteriorating corpse.

Despite the facial decay, it was someone Victor immediately recognized. Dressed in a cheap pirate ensemble, just as Victor saw him last, Karina's friend Damon lay already rotting within the coffin. As much as the seasoned knight didn't like the boy, whatever happened to Damon, he never would have wished this fate upon anyone.

Victor, having been trained in the application of combat medicine over a number of years, inspected the unfortunate soul. A quick scan revealed an absence of stabbing or puncture wounds. External bleeding was not evident on his clothing or flesh. But it was the look on the boy's face that offered volumes of information and required no special training to interpret.

Horror. Pure horror had been molded upon his face. Even after death his hollow eyes (what were left of them) remained fixed wide open, conveying extreme shock and fear, most likely only moments before his demise.

Damon had died of fright.

Victor dropped to a knee and sighed, removing his helm. As much as he wanted to remove Damon from this realm of evil – assuming he could actually find a way out – he would have to come back for him later. Much of his hope in finding Karina had faded. If Damon had died, then odds were Karina suffered the same fate.

But no, he couldn't think like that. And until he could prove Karina's demise, he would remain steadfast in finding her, hoping against hope that she somehow avoided Damon's lot.

For now, Victor would offer a quiet prayer for God's mercy upon Damon's soul. He struggled for the right words, not because of what he thought about Damon but because of the burden upon him and the corrupt environment, as if an unseen dark presence weighed heavily on him, disrupting his very thoughts. Despair itself attacked him, evidence of his sorrow for Damon and worry for the princess, but through will and determination he concluded his prayer for Damon with an Amen.

Victor stood up and donned his helm, turning his attention to the headstone. Grabbing the lantern and shining its dim light at the engraving, he witnessed an absence of name, date of birth, and date of death. Jaggedly etched into the stone, it simply read:

"...They went down alive into the realm of the dead, with everything they owned; the earth closed over them, and they perished and were gone..."

Victor's body tensed up. It took him a short moment to recall where he had heard those words, but he had definitely heard them before.

It came to him suddenly as he remembered hearing that verse in a class he had taken during his knighthood training with the church. "Numbers 16," he muttered with a combination of concern and displeasure. "Straight from the Bible." It distressed him how greatly those words had been taken from the most Holy of Books and perverted for evil purposes.

Turning his attention to the grave, even with the lantern's light Victor couldn't tell how deep the grave had been dug. All he could see were four walls of dirt descending into an empty black pit. Picking up a small round pebble from the dirt pile, he tossed it down the hole and, once it vanished from sight, he listened intently with an expectation of hearing it hit the bottom.

But it never made a sound.

Imagining Damon's coffin hurled into an oblivion of endless darkness, the thought of leaving his body behind began to weigh heavily upon his mind. Victor couldn't imagine such desecration – not to anyone.

Returning to the coffin, Victor carefully and respectfully lifted him out with his shield arm, flicking off the maggots, and gently rested his remains over his shoulder. With any luck, he would be able to hide his body somewhere nearby and return shortly after he rescued Karina.

It wasn't far down the foggy pathway when Victor saw the decrepit and discolored grey walls – perhaps walls of white many centuries ago – walls of a hidden mausoleum. It seemed like he had his answer, or at least a temporary solution to his problem at hand.

Carefully working his way around the old structure, he came across a rather large entryway featuring two large angelic statues guarding a granite door. As with the mausoleum, the statues appeared to have been beautiful at one time; immaculate detail was evident in the original sculpting. But after years of erosion from the natural elements, coupled with reprehensible vandalism, they appeared sinister – and almost demonic.

Stonework upon one of the angelic faces had been crudely chipped away forming fanged teeth and jagged cuts at the corners of the mouth, but even more disturbing was the sanded-down eyes and accompanying faded-black tear stains. The other statue's face had been caved in, giving it a hollow and gaunt appearance. Each statue featured an outstretched arm as if beckoning Victor to enter, yet leaving him uncertain if he would ever leave alive.

He slowly climbed up the few steps, his hand resting upon his axe and his head swiveling back and forth from statue to statue, not convinced they weren't up to something ominous. He scoffed at himself for having such thoughts. The very notion was filled with madness--statues that could move, or threaten, perhaps even harm or kill. Yet he knew that thought wouldn't have even occurred to him before he entered the castle, but now nothing would surprise him.

Victor could have sworn that the ill-omened angels were watching every step he took. Their necks seemed to make the slightest of movements, turning as if their very eyes were upon him – all without making a sound. Then again, if there was any movement, it was so subtle that it could have been his imagination.

Despite his preconceived notion of the worst, he made it to the door without incident. At first, the door wouldn't budge open. Victor guessed that it hadn't been opened in decades if not centuries. With his second attempt, he kicked it as hard as he could, forcing it open a few inches but more importantly unjamming it. The bottom of the door scraped against the stone floor, emitting a horrible shriek so loud it could wake the dead. There was no doubt the sound traveled throughout the entire cemetery ward and perhaps half the castle. He winced, knowing he may have drawn unnecessary attention to himself.

Victor carefully lay Damon down on the ground and prayed his body would be safe until he could return. He didn't want to disrupt any of the caskets in the mausoleum so he turned to leave, but as he prepared to exit his ears picked up on a quiet sound, the tic-tocking of an old grandfather clock.

Through the darkness and across the chamber he spotted the time keeper standing ominously tall against the far wall, as if watching over the tombs of the dead. It must have been at least ten feet tall and weighed five times his own weight. Upon closer inspection, Victor realized it was made of the finest and darkest walnut, but in contrast to the masterwork wood, the glass case was cracked and the pendulum hung at an angle, suspended in place, defying gravity. The hands on the clock were frozen at three hours and eight minutes.

Yet he heard the clock continue to tick away, the stroke of each second echoing off the chamber walls, ringing hollow as if counting away the remaining seconds of life itself, each one telling him that he was one tick closer to decay and death itself.

Memento Mori, he thought to himself, remembering the old book in the study.

The face upon the clock featured a moon, blood red and full, indicating where the moon might actually have hung the very night the clock had been broken.

But the hands of the clock – there was something about the position of the hands... the third hour and the eighth minute. Something familiar that he could not recall. He was surprised when he located the initials of the clockmaker, inscribed on the lower part of the clock. J.O.B.

He carefully tried to recollect any last names that may have started with the letter 'B'; perhaps a name from one of the busts in the library? Perhaps one of the paintings? No; nothing was coming to him. He came up empty.

Victor noticed a shadow moving out of the corner of his eye. Without warning, the large grandfather clock began to fall forward – right where Victor was standing.

Caught off guard, he quickly threw his shield up and stepped toward the side, partially deflecting the falling object and moving out of its way just in time, knocked to the ground in the process. But the timepiece partially landed on one of the stone mausoleum caskets, breaking the lid and collapsing an entire side as well as sending up a cloud of dust.

Victor carefully stood up and, after coughing, swatted away the airborne dust particles. He didn't know how it fell over. As far as he could tell there was nothing that should have caused it to tip over.

With the lid cracked and one of the sides of the casket smashed, it was easy to see the skeleton from one of long past lying uncomfortably inside. The skeleton appeared to be wearing the garb of a royal family member although much of the cloth had wasted away due to the passing of time, yet validating Victor's opinion that this was most likely the tomb of the royal family. There was no doubt this unfortunate soul had been a relative of the king, perhaps a son or grandson, maybe even a nephew of high esteem. Interestingly enough the skeleton held a feathered pen in one hand and a scroll in the other.

Victor knew he was grasping at straws at this point, but desperate for any information he gently pried the sheet of vellum paper from the bony fingers. With the utmost of caution to ensure the parchment didn't crumble in his hands, he took his time to carefully unroll the scroll. It read:

Haceldama! We have accepted our thirty pieces of silver and thus we are paying the terrible price for those cursed and bloodstained coins. Terror… terror of which I cannot speak! Eternal dread! There is no reconciliation any longer, there is only suffering. Oh how I would eat away at my flesh to only numb the pain. To gnaw at my arm, to rip the sinews and flesh with my teeth. Would that I could end the everlasting sting!

Victor, having recognized the writing, froze in place. It matched that of the author of the book he read back in the library.

Will someone not save me? Is it not possible? Of course it is not! They are coming for me; I must hide! But hiding will only be in vain for they are always watching. They are staring at me with their red eyes; they know I can see them. I do not know how, but they know. I hear them taunting me… "Every seven years… every seven years," they say, echoing in a chorus of evil.

"Every seven years…"

I close my eyes and I can still see them…

"Every seven years…"

I scream at them, begging for them to go away but they only laugh and continue to torment me

"Every seven years…"

I try to run but they are all around me

"Every seven years…"

There is only one way out

"Bring one to us… EVERY SEVEN YEARS…"

…and bring them we did. One girl, up to the highest bridge – the Bridge of Sacrifice – was delivered every seven years.

It would come.

Devour.

Shake the foundation of the earth.

And after it was done, over the next seven years, we would pretend nothing happened. But it did happen, and we were always reminded. And then the cycle repeated itself as we did it all over again. The screams of the innocents echo inside my head. Can no one see that? The demons around me shriek; their shrill cries mimic that of the young girls taken, one every seven years. They will not stop.

There is only one way to make the screams stop.

To the mausoleum I go; I shall retire early where my soul may rot with my forefathers in dust and ashes, my body to join the worms. Yes, to the place where the worm does not die and the fire does not quench.

And so I now come to the end of this note – my final writing – as I sit in my coffin and prepare to slide closed the lid and lock it from the inside (for I have no key), and thus it shall remain forever closed... I shall breathe my last. As my hope has faded, may these wretched creatures also fade away, and leave me to wither away and die with only regret to keep me company.

So this was the tragic end that the author had faced. Lying himself down in a stone box devoid of light and air, waiting until he could breathe no more, waiting for the Reaper's hand to come take him away. He was so full of despair that he saw only one way out. Victor, full of sorrow, took a look at the skeleton before him and pitied the man.

His story was awful, yet cryptic. And yet despite his tragic suicide, he played his part out of his own free will, and there were many other victims to feel sorrow. Victor narrowed his eyebrows, thinking about the young girls taken as a sacrifice…

Karina!

Surely that was why she was here! Princess Karina was to become a sacrifice of some sort. She was connected to whatever dark power had seized her. Perhaps she could be found near what the author referenced as the Bridge of Sacrifice, supposedly the highest bridge in the castle. Where could such a bridge be located? If the highest part of a castle were the tower tops, then the bridge was likely at the highest point between the two highest towers.

That was where he must go.

He was in a hurry to leave, but there remained one more thing weighing heavily on his mind, something that still kept nagging at him.

J.O.B. The initials of the clockmaker.

Take away the punctuation and it became "Job". A job. Defined as "To work". That didn't make any sense either. Unless. Of course. The book of the Holy Bible. Job?

Think, Victor... think, he chided himself. But if it was the book of the Bible, there wasn't a verse or a chapter to reference.

Pondering the mystery of the clock, he lowered his head and closed his eyes. This was important because it was connected to Karina. He wasn't sure how, but he just knew it. As random as the events in the castle may have appeared, he was convinced something had been guiding him since he first crossed the threshold of the castle gates. But for good or ill, he couldn't be sure.

He briefly opened his eyes. He happened to be staring down at the face of the clock, its hands still frozen at eight minutes past three.

Three hours and eight minutes.

Of course!

It *was* in fact a Bible verse! Job 3:8!

Victor paused for a moment to recall the Bible verse. *"May those who curse days curse that day, those who are ready to rouse Leviathan."*

In cold silence, all he could do was blink.

The Leviathan... a mighty and ancient creature of untold power, destined to come from the sea. It was said that only the great and powerful sword of God would slay it. He went on to recall other verses about the Leviathan: *"When it rises up, the mighty are terrified; they retreat before its thrashing. The sword that reaches it has no effect, nor does the spear or the dart or the javelin. Iron it treats like straw and bronze like rotten wood."*

Whatever dark forces were unrelentingly sustaining Castle Wraithfall must have been preparing to rouse the Leviathan. And Princess Karina appeared to be its next sacrifice.

Victor ran as fast as he could throughout the castle, giving up his former prudence and ways of caution for the sake of time, for the hourglass would soon run out. As he ran down hall after hall he looked outside through several windows until finally spotting across the way what he believed to be the two largest towers of the castle, both of which were connected hundreds and hundreds of feet high by a stone bridge. He was confident it was there that Karina could be found.

Once inside the tower he climbed stair after stair, his weapon drawn and ready. Up the countless stairs he went until he finally reached the top. And there in front of him, at the stair's end, sat a black, iron door.

Throwing the door open he was immediately met with a gusty wind which nearly knocked him down the shaft of the tower. His back foot slipped off the edge, but he fell sideways, catching himself on the stairs. He pulled himself up and breathed a huge sigh of relief after looking down into the black pit of the stairwell some hundreds of feet below. Angry with himself, he realized his impatience almost cost him his life. Victor entered the room with a restored sense of caution.

The large circular area featured numerous open windows spaced evenly around the room (with exception of the door he came through and the door on the opposite end of the room which led to the bridge), perhaps contributing to the initially massive gust. He suspected the higher altitude might have also accounted for stronger winds, yet strangely, of the hundreds of black candles scattered throughout not a single one had been blown out.

In the center of the room a young woman stood with her back toward Victor, gracefully holding one of the black iron rails of the canopy bed. Her long, elegant and nearly transparent robe flowed hypnotically with the breeze.

She turned around…

"Princess Karina!"

Victor could hardly believe it was her! He almost ran to her, desiring to embrace and comfort her… until she spoke.

"You finally came," she said with an air of confidence, perhaps almost with a touch of smugness. Slowly she glided toward Victor, one foot in front of the other.

Something wasn't right. "Princess Karina? What…"

He noticed there was something different about her, and as she came closer he became more and more convinced she wasn't acting like herself.

"Yes, my love? Have you come to claim your reward?" Her smile was too perfect. She should have been terrified. Yet Karina remained not only calm, but there was an unnerving manner with which she carried herself. It was almost eerie.

Slowly and seductively she began to open her robe. For a moment Victor was lost on her body as she displayed her finest assets, causing him to lower his weapon and shield. He could feel his inhibitions drifting away. His mind was finally beginning to accept this was no longer the child princess, for she was fully an adult.

But, if he had to reveal his greatest secret, the one he had wrestled with only recently… a secret so overwhelming that he buried his own feelings so far down that not even he could recognize it – it was that he wanted more than her body. He wanted *her*.

All of her.

He couldn't explain why or how, but a wave of lust swept over him with such intensity that he felt weak in the legs. The desire he felt was real and passionate, but it was almost unnatural.

She was so much more than the princess, more than beauty. She was a precious friend, a caring companion. And as such, he looked away from her body… and into her eyes. At first, they sparkled with the same crystalline blue he was familiar with. But there was something unusual about her eyes, just unusual enough to convince him they were not those of his Princess Karina.

A violent sickness dropped him to his knees as he realized her eyes weren't actually blue – how he did not notice before, he wasn't sure – but they were pitch black, as black as the moonless night, radiating an evil unlike anything he had ever felt or experienced. They were empty. Soulless. Yet had he been unable to pry his eyes away from her body, he may never have even noticed.

"You kneel before me? That is good… and most wise," she said haughtily, patiently circling around him.

Victor could feel blood rising in his throat; with a single cough, a small splattering lurched out of his mouth and hit the floor. A small drop hung from his lip, elongating into a thin but larger drop. His bones ached and his muscles grew weak. He couldn't even bring himself to stand in the presence of such evil.

"Y-you… you're n-not the princess," he strained out. "Wh..who are…"

"Come now," she scoffed. "I am whoever you want me to be. I can take any form you desire. And this one seems to be to your liking, no?" Gradually she lowered the robe past her shoulders.

This was all wrong. He tried to pray… he tried to utter the name of Jesus on his lips, but it wouldn't come. He couldn't say his Savior's name. A single tear dripped down to the floor, followed by another, and then another. He was horrified as he realized they were tears of blood; his very eyes were bleeding.

The timing of her laughter was uncanny. Victor wondered if she knew what he was doing.

Victor knew that even if he couldn't say the name of Jesus with his tongue, he could say it in his heart. "Christ is King… Christ is King…" he repeated over and over in his mind, refusing to be overcome.

The false Karina laughed even louder. The sound of a young woman intertwined with a deep guttural growl escaping from her lips echoed throughout the tower.

Bearing row upon row of razor-sharp teeth, her mouth unnaturally widened and a hideous sound came out. "THERE IS NO GOD HERE, SLAVE," the demonic voice hissed.

Victor prayed in his mind even harder. He couldn't stand. He couldn't grasp his weapon. Sweat rolled off his brow and blood still trickled out of his mouth and eyes.

Her voice and mouth returned to normal as if never distorted in the first place, and she let out a soft giggle. "But fortunately for you, I am the only one you need." She offered a fake lament, bending down behind him and whispering in his ear, "Aww. You look to be in a dreadful amount of pain and suffering. And the pain will not end any time soon. You may die here from the pain, perhaps from starvation. Or perhaps your bones will wax old, wasting into nothing, or your body will simply wither away."

With a twisted smile, she added, "But I can restore you."

Though it took all of his strength, Victor managed to lift his head. The pain was tremendous. He could barely tolerate it any longer. It was as much of a mental struggle as it was physical. The temptation to give in to her, to allow her to ease the pain, was great.

Yet he couldn't give in, not like that. Though there may be great pain to him, he would not betray his God. Despite his suffering, even as blood dripped down off his tongue, he spoke with confidence, "The scripture says, *"Look at the birds of the air; they do not sow or reap or store away in barns, and yet your heavenly Father feeds them. Are you not much more valuable than they?"* So my answer is no, monster. I refuse your help and choose to rely on my Lord's hand of providence, despite your dark curse upon me."

"You underestimate my power. I will not only heal you, but I offer you riches beyond your wildest dreams," she exclaimed. "You could rule as king with tens of wives at your side, hundreds of mistresses for companionship, thousands of servants to do your bidding, and hundreds of thousands of loyal soldiers for your personal army. Imagine storehouses of grain and gold… all for you. You have only to take my hand, and you shall rule the world."

The unyielding concentrated evil seemed to be spreading within him and attacking the purity of his very soul. And moreover, it was as if a fog permeated his mind, but he continued praying in his heart. Yet for all his turmoil, Victor somehow found the strength to counter and said, "It is written, *"Do not store up for yourselves treasures on earth, where moths and vermin destroy, and where thieves break in and steal. But store up for yourselves treasures in heaven, where moths and vermin do not destroy, and where thieves do not break in and steal. For where your treasure is, there your heart will be also."*

The wind blew harder and the candles flickered rapidly, as if the very air around him grew angry. She spoke again, but her laughter had been replaced with a spewing venomous wrath. "There is only one way your princess can be spared from the Leviathan, and only one way you shall survive. Allow me into your life, and let me watch over your family line for generations to come. This is all I ask. Forsake your Creator and take my hand. This is the only way her life shall be spared. Otherwise a horrible and gruesome death is upon both of your heads."

"Death?" Victor shook his head. "You still do not understand. Long ago three devout followers of the Lord, upon facing persecution and death, said to their king, *If we are thrown into the blazing furnace, the God we serve is able to deliver us from it, and he will deliver us from Your Majesty's hand. But even if he does not, we want you to know, Your Majesty, that we will not serve your gods or worship the image of gold you have set up.* And thrown into the furnace they were. And that day, the Lord chose to deliver them."

Despite his agony, Victor managed a smile and said, "I will love Karina more than you will ever know. But I trust…" He took a breath, groaned and then with all of his might forced out, "I trust the Christ." Clenching his teeth, determined to follow in the footsteps of the prophets before him, he grunted out, "I… choose fire!"

Enraged, she yelled at the top of her lungs, and then her face slowly altered, displaying a sunken gaunt and pale scowl. Suddenly the room erupted with what he could only describe as a wave of dark energy; he was hit in the chest so hard that it felt as if his heart would explode.

Yet it came to pass, and within mere seconds she was nowhere to be seen and the light of every candle had been snuffed out. The room was dark and empty, abandoned, but it remained untouched.

It was almost as if what had just transpired had never really happened.

Victor still felt the pain in his body and soul though, assuring him that whatever had happened was real enough. After taking a few breaths, the pain subsided just enough for him to function. He took a quick moment to bow his head and once more thank his God. Though his body ached and the very fiber of his core felt weak, his renewed faith energized him.

Warily he grasped his axe and brought one knee forward. Steadfast, he pushed off of the ground and forced himself to his feet, ready to carry on.

Victor walked across the room, held his breath and carefully pushed open the door leading to the bridge.

A large grey bridge, connecting one tower to the next, lay before him. He was surprised at the sheer size of the bridge. When he first laid eyes upon it from far away it didn't seem impressive. But up close, Victor could now see that the span was enormous. Solid stone railings adorned each side, rising up to the waist-level. Victor guessed the sturdy bridge was several hundred feet long, and perhaps four times as high. About half way down the bridge he noticed a large wooden frame in the shape of an "X" bolted down to the stone bridge floor.

Standing up against the obscene wooden device was Princess Karina.

His heart skipped a beat. On one hand he was relieved to see her – he had finally found Karina. On the other hand, given the cryptic prophecy of what her fate was to become, a heavy fear came over him.

Four iron chains dangled from each end, ensuring her wrists and ankles were held firmly in place. She was still dressed in her All Hallows Eve costume, but it was evident that she had been treated roughly as proven by the multiple scratches and tears in what little fabric there was. There were also marks upon her body. Cuts and bruises marked her skin and a thin trail of blood ran down her leg. A cloth gag prevented her from effectively crying out for help, but her muffled screams could still be heard. Her cries for help were directed toward Victor.

The moment she made eye contact with him, it was as if the world stopped if for only a moment. This was his Karina, the real princess.

Yet despite her trepidation and tear-stained face, she now displayed a tremendous amount of relief in seeing her protector, knowing that he had finally come. For her. The princess tried to shout something to him, but it was unintelligible because of her gag. She tugged fiercely at her chains. Victor wasted no time in running to her.

Her eyes immediately met his, and if there had been any doubt of their feelings before it was immediately erased. Their personal admissions didn't have long, however. An ear-shattering noise erupted from the ocean below.

Victor dared to look over the stone railing and down toward the ocean.

Rising up from the depths of the ocean, a winged monstrosity much like a gliding serpent took to the night sky, shrieking once again.

It was the Leviathan.

Everything that the long deceased author spoke of was now happening. It was the seventh year, and the massive creature had returned. And this time Karina was the sacrifice.

Victor immediately swung his axe at one of the chains holding her wrist. She let out a muffled scream. Without hesitation he struck again and again, unleashing a myriad of sparks, until the chain severed. Quickly he hit the chain holding her other wrist, this time striking faster and breaking it with two solid blows.

Karina didn't stop screaming. Even without turning around he was aware the monster from the abyss was flying toward them with great haste.

With her hands free, she pulled off her gag and screamed, "Victor! It's almost here!" He frantically swung at her ankle chain and smashed it with multiple strikes.

There was one last chain. He glanced up. The Leviathan was almost upon them. Its speed was incredible. He didn't think he could free her in time. It drew its head back. Its maw gaped in anticipation. Victor's eyes opened wide with the realization that the monster's throat was a blazing furnace. Flames rose inside its mouth and the heat convection blurred like a hideous mirage.

The monster inhaled, fanning its own flames, smoke smoldering in its mouth and nostrils.

With one mighty swing, Victor severed the last chain. He grabbed Karina and threw her to the ground and up against the stone rail just as a concentrated blast of flame ignited the wooden structure where she had been a mere second before.

Karina struggled to get away, terrified, but Victor held her in place. The heat was so intense the metal from his armor began to burn his skin. He clenched his jaw and swore to withstand the pain for as long as it took.

The flame stopped as the Leviathan landed on the stone rail, fracturing the solid structure with its claws. Victor grabbed Karina by the arm and ran toward the tower.

The creature struck, its neck jutting out and rows of razor-sharp teeth snapping at Victor. Its underside was jagged like steel potsherds, easily capable of slicing flesh and bone, but Victor was ready, looking over his shoulder as he ran and never letting it out of his sight. With a counterstrike, Victor swung his axe and blocked with his shield. His axe bounced off the monsters scales. He marveled at how the creature's natural armor was as hard as iron. With his shield he managed to deflect the teeth, but the sheer power from the head of the beast dented his shield and knocked Victor over.

"Run!" He blurted toward Karina. Dazed, he tried to regain his footing.

Karina stopped and ran back to his side. "Victor!"

He couldn't believe his eyes. He screamed at her, "No! You Run!"

"I'm not leaving you, Victor!"

The creature prepared to strike again.

"I can't hold him! My death will be in vain!"

"Victor! No! You go. It wants me!"

His frustration grew.

"I swore an oath."

A powerful claw swung at Victor. He ducked. It smashed more of the rail.

Karina shouted at him, "Victor, I'm ordering you to leave!"

Victor had no choice but to ignore her. The creature was simply too fast, and leaving her behind wasn't an option. But the field of battle was his expertise, and his one advantage. Analyzing the situation around him, he had one idea that might work.

The creature drew its head back once again. Victor could feel the air around him heating up intensely. He could see a raging inferno rising in its throat. Taking his axe with two hands and winding his arms back, he stepped forward and heaved it as hard as he could at one of the feet clutching the stone rail. Victor knew it wouldn't penetrate its armor, but it wasn't meant to. It was hardly a glancing blow, but the force of the throw was enough to cause the Leviathan to shift its massive weight and in doing so, the perch beneath crumbled, causing the beast to plummet below.

Without wasting time, Victor grabbed her arm and, dragging her in tow, ran toward the tower. He muttered, "Don't even *think* of giving me an order right now. Especially one as absurd as that."

A comment like that would have normally infuriated her and ensured such a rude individual would be placed in the stocks for a week, yet ironically it caused a soft, tiny smile to rise upon Karina's lips. Only Victor could get away with addressing her in such a tone, and only in this moment of life and death.

"I'll never let you go," he said quietly, so quiet in fact that she wasn't sure if she was supposed to have heard.

"That winged monster will return," Victor said, just before another screech from below confirmed his statement.

Quickly they entered the tower and scrambled down the winding stairs.

A terrible crash impacted the side of the tower. Looking up through one of the small stairwell windows, they could both see the Leviathan hadn't given up. The creature slammed the tower again and again. Dust was shaken from the walls, and even a few stones had come loose.

Karina held his hand tightly, trying not to fall as they ran down the awkward stairs. She made the mistake of looking down the tower shaft and into the darkness below, making her dizzy and reminding her how high up the tower they truly were.

With each powerful slam, both Victor and Karina held their breath, hoping the tower would remain intact long enough for them to reach the bottom.

Another devastating hit caved in part of the tower wall, forming a large hole. It wasn't big enough for the Leviathan to come through yet. Large stone fragments fell below. Victor came to a sudden stop, but Karina didn't. Quickly he wrapped his arms around her and yanked her back just as a solid rectangular stone fell from above, smashing the stairs in front of them, leaving a large gap.

"We have to jump," Victor told her.

Karina's tears were flowing once more. She was petrified with fear. Victor didn't blame her; she was young and untrained, and their situation was dire. But she wasn't a soldier he could yell and motivate with force. She was tender. Delicate. She was a princess.

Carefully lifting his visor, he took his hands to her cheeks, making sure her eyes could see his. "I need you to make this jump," he said calmly.

Her lip quivered and she shook her head.

"You can do this, but you have to do it now. I'll be right behind you." Again Victor spoke calmly, although everything inside him was screaming for him to keep moving. The tower was still being torn apart and they didn't have much longer.

"I've seen you jump horses to heights and distances greater than most of my men. I've seen you dance, jumping from the tips of your toes. Look at me… you can do this. Don't be scared. I'm here with you."

He began to see that fighting spirit in her eyes once again. She was beginning to trust him. The princess nodded. Turning toward the stairs across the gap, Karina took a deep breath. Victor placed his hands upon her hips and said, "On three. One… two… THREE!"

Karina jumped and Victor boosted her across the gap. She safely made it the full distance, but landed hard on the other side. Nonetheless she was safe.

Victor immediately jumped after her, but as he landed, the stair he came to rest on crumbled underneath his feet. He quickly scrambled forward, grabbing the next stair with his hands before he could fall into the darkness below.

"Victor!"

She lurched forward and grabbed his arms. "Run!" was all he said to her.

She held on as tightly as she could, aware that the Leviathan would penetrate the tower within moments. Straining to pull him up, she told him, "We've been over this. I'm not going anywhere without you!" It took every ounce of strength she had, but she managed to help Victor up. He didn't say a word, but there was something about the look on his face that captured her attention. Once again, he took her hand and led her down the stairs.

The Leviathan made it inside the tower just as Victor and Karina reached the bottom of the tower. With a terrifying scream, the creature dove straight down the center of the tower. Victor opened the door and pushed Karina through, following behind her and slamming it closed, just moments before the horrific creature could reach them.

With one final scream, the Leviathan launched upward and out of their sight. The tower had finally stopped shaking, and all was quiet.

***

Victor and Karina could breathe a little easier now that they were back within the castle's walls and away from the monstrous creature, but they still had to find a way out.

"Maybe whatever that was gave up chasing after me?" Karina asked as he dragged her along.

"Maybe," Victor said, not convinced that was the case. He took a brief moment to stop, but delayed in letting go of her hand. He still had to get her out of the castle, yet the fact that she was with him gave him new reserves of energy. Not knowing if she was dead or alive was the most painful experience he ever had to endure.

"I-forgive me, Your Highness. Are you all right? Wait, let me get some bandages." He began to inspect her more closely, stopping at the thin blood trail on her leg.

"I'll be fine. Let's just get out of here first. Okay? It only hurts a little, and it will not slow me down."

Victor knew she was right and that they had to keep moving. He reluctantly nodded, turning to face the hallway and decipher the best way out of the castle.

"Wait," she said anxiously. "I'm so, so sorry," she whispered.

At first Victor didn't know what to say, but then he stepped forward and held her close. Gently he brought her head to his armored chest and kissed the top of her head through her golden curls. "You don't need to apologize, princess. This is a terrible place of evil and you were in the wrong place at the wrong time. This is not your fault."

Squeezing her eyes shut, she nodded and said, "Yes it is! If I-if I didn't…"

Victor cut her off and shushed her. He simply held her.

Wrapping her arms around his neck, Karina closed her eyes and pursed her lips, inches away from his.

Before their lips could touch, a deafening sound from outside the castle walls startled them and shook the castle windows.

Frightened, Karina flinched. Victor instinctively pulled away, turning his attention outside the castle.

"That dragon-creature! Is he trying to break into the castle now? I don't see anything."

Victor replied, "No, that sound…it sounded like the ocean erupted. My instincts tell me it returned to the dark aquatic abyss." He took a moment to ponder why the creature had given up so easily when, if given enough time, it could have leveled the castle.

For a brief moment, everything was calm.

But then, the very ground beneath their feet began to violently shake as a powerful shockwave, or perhaps an earthquake, tore throughout the castle, shattering the windows with the force of an eruption. Both of them were thrown off balance.

Victor, after regaining his steadiness, grabbed her hand and ran down the corridor.

It was as if the castle was alive, its stone walls trying to keep them inside so it could swallow them whole.

"What is happening?" Princess Karina screamed, watching part of the ceiling collapse.

"Since the Leviathan failed to take you, I am guessing it was a violation of the Pact, forcing the termination of the agreement. And it would seem that results in the absolute destruction of Wraithfall Castle, which we are now trapped in. And I sense that it doesn't want to let us go. It wants to bury us with it."

Victor attempted to navigate his way through the crumbling castle. A large section of floor buckled behind Princess Karina, causing her to lose her footing. Victor, still holding her hand, forcefully pulled her up and continued running before it could claim them both.

Sprinting through one of the main dining rooms, the chandelier crashed on the table next to the couple. Victor held his shield up in front of Princess Karina, deflecting crystal shards and splinters of debris before continuing.

Further down the hallway, one of the walls collapsed just before they entered, forcing them to take another route.

The foundation of the entire castle continued to shake. Victor and the princess finally found themselves at a dead-end in an old embattlement and at the end of their exhausting run.

Longbows, crossbows, countless arrows and even an old rope littered the room and had been untouched for some time. A large iron cauldron, once used to pour scalding hot oil on opposing enemies (though it was now empty), had been tipped over, most likely during the castle's violent swan song.

A small section of wall where one of the narrow arrow slits had been was missing; Victor suspected the cauldron might have been violently thrown against the wall during the earthquake.

Karina, looking through the hole in the wall to the outside, excitedly tugged his arm and said, "Victor! I see people down there!"

Victor took a look down below. It was a good thirty-foot drop, but more importantly he recognized the terrain as the front of the castle. It was the same place where he led his soldiers on an assault.

He breathed a heavy sigh of relief upon realizing the people down below were the very same soldiers. Karina had been right! His relief turned to sadness as he realized how few remained.

"Sergeant Aldergrove!" Victor shouted below, waving his arms.

The Sergeant, in disbelief, saw him and flagged down several of the other soldiers. "Look up, third story," he shouted to the others, pointing toward Victor and Princess Karina.

It was a long way down, Victor thought. Taking a quick look around the room, he grabbed the rope and sized it up. "Forty to fifty feet. This should work," he said to no one in particular. He took one end of the rope and began to wrap it around the princess.

Realizing what he was doing, she said, "Wait! Victor, how are you going to get down if you send me down with the rope?"

Victor looked at her briefly, and shouted, "Sergeant, I'm going to lower Princess Karina to you. Get ready!"

"No. Wait, just stop! Tie the rope off to something and we can both go down it!"

Victor shook his head and said, "I've already thought of that. There is nothing I can tie it to. Even if there was, the entire castle is ready to collapse and we don't have time. I will hold it myself, serving as your anchor so I can lower you down."

"There has to be another way! There has to," Princess Karina cried.

Victor had already begun to push her toward the opening in the wall. "You'll be safe, Princess."

It amazed him how much Karina resisted, for she knew the same cold hard fact as he. There was no way out for him. But that was acceptable because it was his job. He was the protector of the Princess of Shandwick, and by his sacrifice she would be safe.

Yet she struggled and fought back as if the very fall would kill her. She pleaded, "No, *don't do this*!" Victor could barely look into her eyes. They were the eyes of one who had been betrayed by a friend. She screamed with desperation, "Victor! I'm commanding you to stop! Victor!"

"Forgive me. I am not in the habit of ignoring the commands of my beloved princess, but for your own safety I have no choice."

Despite his strength, Victor tried to hoist her up and through the hole, but she fought back desperately. "Please! You're running out of time! Stop fighting me, princess!"

"NO!"

He was exasperated. She wouldn't listen to reason. As he stopped trying to force her out, she immediately clung to him, holding him tightly as if her life depended on it.

A loud thunderous rumble echoed not too far away. He realized an entire section of the castle had collapsed, and by the sound of it, fallen into the ocean. They were almost out of time.

He took a deep breath, placed two fingers underneath her chin and gently lifted it until she looked at him.

"Karina," he said in a soft voice.

"But you also said you would never let me go! You promised me."

"I-I'm sorry," he choked, trying to hold his own emotions back. "I suppose I did. It saddens me to break that promise."

He sighed. At a loss for words, he could only tell her the cruel truth. "I have no choice. I have to let you go now." Tilting her head back, he placed his lips upon hers, knowing it would be their first kiss… and their last. If either of them could have stopped time, it would have been frozen in that single moment forever. She kissed him back fiercely, placing her hands alongside his head, her tears dampening his cheeks; he kissed her back just as passionately, wrapping his hands around her slender waist.

With terrible remorse, he swept her legs out from under her and, still holding the rope, carried her to the edge. Realizing what he had planned, she wrapped her arms around him tightly and refused to be let go.

"No! If you can't come with me, I'm not leaving! I'm staying with you!"

"It's time, Karina," he said, begrudgingly prying her off. Desperately she grabbed at his hand as he lowered her though the makeshift window.

The sorrow on her face hurt Victor more than anything else, especially after he pried her fingers off, effectively letting go of her hand.

"*I love you*! Please, don't do this, Victor! Please! I love you!"

Victor couldn't speak. He simply focused on lowering her hand over hand, professions of her love echoing inside his head, making sure she made it down safely. Before her feet touched the ground, Sergeant Aldergrove and three of his men grabbed her and ran from the disintegrating castle.

They hadn't taken more than a few steps when the entire structure of Wraithfall Castle gave way. Half of the castle crashed into the ocean while the other half fell to the ground, causing an eruption of dust and debris hundreds of feet into the air, no doubt heard miles and miles away.

Sergeant Aldergrove barked, "Keep running!" He held up his shield to protect the princess from falling debris and forceful waves from the black cloud of stone. She remained inconsolable, oblivious to the immediate danger around her.

Once they were a safe distance away and the dust had settled, he instructed the remaining soldiers to take the princess back to the castle, ensuring her protection at all costs. Turning toward the pile of rubble, he asked for a few volunteers to stay behind and help him find their commander. No one was ever left behind. Dead or alive, Victor would be brought back home.

***

Darkness.

And then voices.

At first, he couldn't make out specific words or identities. Maybe they were the angels of God, preparing to bring him home. If he were to pass through the Gates of Heaven and kneel before the throne of God, he could only pray to be found worthy in the eyes of the Lord.

How he longed to hear, "Well done, good and faithful servant," knowing he answered the calling and served Him well.

His eyes were closed, yet it seemed bright all around him. It was a phenomenon that he couldn't explain. But then for a brief moment, he could have sworn he heard soldiers calling to him. Perhaps they were the ones slain in battle such as he had been, preparing to enter the Kingdom of Heaven along his side. And then, there was nothing.

***

"Sergeant! Over here," one of the soldiers cried out enthusiastically.

Sergeant Aldergrove ran across the field of debris, finding a small crowd of men surrounding a large, iron cauldron of some sort. At the base of the cauldron rested a familiar shield.

His eyes began to open, but because it was so bright he could only squint.

Pain registered. Incredible amounts of agony. He didn't know where he was, but it couldn't have been heaven… not with suffering like this.

He was vaguely aware of groaning, but where it came from he had no idea. It could have been from his own lips for all he knew. A calm and soothing voice began to speak. He couldn't tell what was being said, but there was beauty behind it, and somehow it gave him peace.

Once again, he slipped away, likely to forget about what had just transpired. Images from another time played inside his head, scenes unfolding from the past. Children ran around in the schoolyard; all of the boys pretending to be knights chased an imaginary dragon, which apparently had just escaped the school's boundaries. A new act quickly followed. This time he saw a young boy, or perhaps a young man in his mid to late teens, standing in front of the double doors of the training academy inside the church. The young man awkwardly held a large sack over his shoulder – filled with books, judging by the rectangular forms stretching out the bag – but in his free hand he held a teddy bear.

Bending down on one knee, the young man offered the stuffed animal to a little girl who was clearly sad to see him go. But he knew what the young man was thinking. He was sad, too, but it was time to go. While the mother scooped up the little girl, who was on the verge of tears, the father gently smiled and, with a firm grip, he shook the teenager's hand.

***

Fingertips lightly stroked his forehead, and he didn't want to wake up. At first, it felt wonderful, but then his own body betrayed him, reminding him of the pain radiating from head to toe.

"Don't move," he heard a voice gently say, presumably the same person touched his forehead. "Try to remain still. It will hurt less."

He knew that voice. That sweet, soothing voice. Karina's, of course.

"Where…" he wheezed, barely able to speak.

"Shhh," she tenderly chastised him, "Don't try to speak. Just rest. You've been through a lot."

His eyes began to flutter open. He tried to shift his body but a sharp pain in his left leg warned him otherwise.

Karina winced, "See? I told you not to move! You're so stubborn sometimes!"

Victor began to laugh, but he cut it short when his chest hurt. Fractured or broken ribs, he suspected. Still, he managed to control his breathing, just to tell her, "Stubborn? Who do you think I learned from?"

Now fully awake, he noticed the smile on her face. She was beaming, smiling from ear to ear. Her eyes sparkled. "You scared me. You scared me badly," she whispered, her smile fading away, replaced with a look of worry.

He reached out to her and, with his gauntlet now removed, his bare fingertips caressed the side of her face. It was nice to touch her. It reminded him that she was alive. He – and the entire kingdom, of course – came *so* incredibly close to losing her.

Just as quickly as her sadness came, it vanished, replaced with a blush.

He removed his hand quickly, afraid he had gone too far. But she didn't say anything.

"So, what happened? My memory isn't completely clear. The last thing I remember was lowering you down the rope."

Princess Karina pursed her lips and narrowed her eyebrows. Clearly, Victor thought, forcing her down the rope was still a sore subject. But she moved past her anger and said, "Only seconds after I made it to the ground the entire castle collapsed. Some of the soldiers stayed behind to search for you." She began to choke up as she said, "I-I thought y-you were-were, dead." Taking a deep breath, she recovered and said, "Don't ever do that to me again!"

He pondered her words carefully, trying to recreate the scene in his mind. "I should have been killed. How did I survive?"

Regaining her composure, she told him, "Do you remember the room we were in? Do you remember that large cauldron? Apparently you jumped inside it before the castle collapsed. It saved you from being crushed, but obviously the fall was still a long way down." She smiled, "At least you are alive. I saw the castle fall. I didn't think…"

One of the doctors came up to the two and, after humbly bowing, said, "Princess Karina? Please forgive me, your highness, but now that Sir Victor is awake--"

She interrupted with a sigh. "I know, I know," she said, keeping her eyes on Victor. She stood up, getting ready to leave and told Victor, "Time to rest. I'll come back every day. I promise." Without hesitation, regardless of witnesses in the room, she leaned down and tenderly kissed him on the lips.

While somewhat shocked by her actions and worried about improper perception, he didn't try to stop her.

***

After too many days of bed rest, Victor was finally able to move around, albeit with assistance from a wooden cane. But the absence of armor for the first time since he entered Wraithfall Castle helped. He was told his leg was healing well, and if he continued to make progress he would soon be able to walk unassisted.

Many from his Order had come by to check on him and congratulate him for saving Karina. The princess, however, had visited him every single day just as she promised. But today, he was hoping to return the favor with a surprise visit.

He found her in the flower garden sitting on a sculpted ivory bench surrounded by her Ladies-in-Waiting, one of which held the end of her long flowing dress to keep it out of the fresh morning dew.

Her laughter captivated him and brought a smile to his face. He delayed approaching her, fearing her beautiful and infectious smile might fade away. Whatever they were all laughing about didn't matter. What did matter was the fact that she was alive and full of happiness. He was once again reminded how close he had come to losing her. That thought was unbearable.

But here she was, clothed in the finest of royal dresses, her crown upon her head just as it should be. It was an encouraging – and beautiful – portrait.

His heart skipped a beat the moment her eyes caught his. Her smile instantly grew even bigger. Quickly she stood up and, without warning, ran across the garden and threw her arms around him.

Victor laughed, although he had to make a concentrated effort to keep his balance.

"You're on your feet again! I knew you would be," she said, and seemed to glow in the sunlight.

"I just wanted to check up on you," he smiled back. "It's become habit after all of these years. I almost didn't know what to do without you. Is your new knight protector treating you well?"

With a stern look, she corrected him, "*Temporary* protector. And yes, she's fine. But you'll be back in no time!"

A guilty look crossed his face, which didn't escape her notice.

"What is it?"

He wasn't sure how to tell her. It wasn't going to be easy. "I have to step down."

She looked like she had been slapped in the face.

"What?"

"I have to step down. As much as I want to remain your protector, I, well, I failed to protect you. And that failure almost cost your life. I know we briefly discussed this before you were taken. If anything, the fact that you were captured right under my very nose is proof enough. I'm to meet with the king and queen later today, and I am giving them my resignation.   Quite honestly, I expected them to release me already, but it seems they stayed their hand until I could properly heal. Your parents always were fair and kind, and to that I owe them my gratitude."

Her mouth hung open, but no words came out. "I- no! You can't."

"It's not that simple," he sighed. A shade of red crept up on his face as he said, "Plus, I may have, as you recall... taken... inappropriate actions with you."

The worry on her face gradually morphed to a look of amusement. "You mean when you kissed me?"

Victor offered a defeated smile and said, "Losing my job or even having my knighthood stripped away is the least of my concerns, compared to what the king and queen might do."

He was surprised she seemed so calm.

"Well, if you must know – not to ruin the surprise – I spoke with my parents several days ago about this very subject." She sheepishly added, "They knew I may have been slightly defiant with you in the days that led up to my disappearance."

"Slightly?"

"Hush, you. As I was saying, they understand I put you in a horrible situation. And I confessed that to them. But I was adamant that, after all I put you through, they keep you as my knight protector. But I made them promise not to say anything to you, because I wanted to be the one to tell you first."

Victor sighed. He was caught in a quandary, and she knew it.

"But still, even if they were to retain me, the honorable thing is to step down."

"After all we've been through, you would still consider leaving me? Just like that?"

Princess Karina batted her eyes. He suspected she was using her charms against him intentionally. And he was irritated that it seemed to be working.

She continued, "Did I ever tell you my first memory of you? You were so kind and sweet. And I don't remember why, but you gave me that little stuffed teddy bear. Do you remember?"

Of course he remembered. He nodded.

She laughed. "That was also the day I knew we were going to get married."

He recoiled. With great surprise and discomfort, he retorting, "You were four!"

She snapped, "No. I was *five!* And you were just a boy yourself then." Her voice softened, "You've always held a special place in my heart. You meant so much more to me than you could possibly imagine. I remember being sad after that, because you went off to your Knighthood training with the church. But then you came back, and I was so excited! And ever since, you've been watching over me. Protecting me."

Karina smiled, "I still have that bear, you know." Victor smiled warmly. He knew she was pulling on his heartstrings, conjuring up old memories, simply to convince him to remain her protector.

"That reminds me," Victor said, pulling something out of his pocket. She leaned back to see what he held in his hand.

"Something else that belongs to you. A silver cross necklace."

She gasped and covered her mouth.

He gently moved her hair aside, grazing his fingertips across her neck as he fastened the necklace around her neck for a second time.

"Really, princess. You must be more careful with your possessions," he teased her.

"I thought it was gone forever. Where did you find it?"

"That's not important," he smiled. "But what is important is what this cross symbolizes. I found it to be a reminder of hope in such a dark, dark place."

Karina wrapped her arms around him. "So nice to feel a man and not an iron breastplate when I hug you," she muttered. She placed her head against his chest and sighed.

Victor smiled and held her back. He realized that her embrace was unnaturally long. He could sense her body wasn't ready to pull away. And he didn't mind. For once, he wasn't concerned with consequences, and it didn't feel wrong.

"This time I mean it," he whispered into her ear. "I'm never letting you go."

She didn't say a word, but he felt her head nodding against his body. Quite possibly, judging by the wet tears on his shoulder, because she was too choked up to speak.

"There is something which we haven't discussed," Victor said sedately, holding her hand while escorting her back to her tower some time later.

"I was wondering if you would bring it up," Karina replied with a very serious look on her face. She stopped on the walkway and placed one hand on the stone rail while her other hand nervously played with the cross hanging from her necklace. Briefly she looked up at the moon while trying to figure out what to say. "Before you ask, I remember hardly anything. But even then, I still remember an evil presence. A stronger evil than I have ever felt in my life, or thought possible." She crossed her arms, as if a cold wave washed across her skin.

Victor didn't say a word. He moved in behind her and gently placed his hands on her shoulder, letting her know it was all right.

The princess continued, "It was as if I was lost in a sleepless nightmare, expecting that I should never awaken." She thought for a moment and then said, "I have so many questions, and I do not know if I want any of them answered. What was that thing? That creature? Why did they want me? I just..."

Victor slid his arms around her, hoping to comfort her. He didn't blame her. The things he saw – they were visions of unclean evil. He had learned much about the history of Castle Wraithfall, but each answer brought about several more questions.

"Will it come back for me?"

Victor thought about The Pact. As near as he could tell, that dark contract had been broken the moment he found and rescued Karina, although who knew how long ago it had been signed and agreed upon. Would the creature return in seven years for a new victim, or was the dark agreement made null? He suspected the later.

"No. I do not believe it will. Yet even if it should return, I will be waiting. And this time, I will not let you out of my sight, not for a single moment."

Karina turned in his arms and looked up at him, allowing herself the smallest of smiles.

And Victor was thankful she did. After all she had been through, she deserved it.

Far below the same pale moon that Princess Karina had gazed upon, yet a great distance away, a wretched old man held aloft his violin bow with knobby fingers before bringing it down across the strings, playing an ominous requiem in the night.

"There will be more," said the strange voice coming out of the old man, "so many more."

Terrible Choices

Patricia Mattern

Patricia Mattern

When a research scientist is abducted by a cartel during a romantic getaway with his wife, he is faced with stunningly terrible choices: will he betray his government to save his family—or save his family and become a traitor? His captors have no idea that he is not as vulnerable as he seems. All his neurons will be working overtime as he outwits his captors and escapes, though not unscathed, from an unthinkable situation.

When consciousness found him, the first thing he was aware of was that his throat was on fire and his tongue was stuck to the roof of his mouth. He could see a pair of expensive looking men's shoes at eye level some distance away across a cream colored carpet. His visual line was partially blocked by something in variegated shades of deep rose and pink that had the look of soft tissue. He could see that it was oozing onto the same carpet that his left cheek was firmly pressed against.

When he tried to get up, he found his hands were trussed behind him.

"Your wife's ovaries," a man's voice intoned from somewhere in the stratosphere above his head. "We took the liberty of having them surgically removed. And unless you tell us everything we want to know about the Haploid Project, we will continue to harvest Marie's nonessential organs with very little recovery time in between surgical procedures…"

Through the fog of whatever substance the Carnetti Crime family had used to drug him, a knifelike pain shot through his core. He and Marie had one son, Colin, back in the U.S. She had been asking him for a brother or sister for Colin repeatedly, but he had demurred, wanting to get the specs on the Haploid Infuser perfect for corporate. His dedication to fringe and futuristic science and delivering a patentable version of the impossible was why they paid him handsomely.

Now Colin would be an only child, *their* only child. The rest of his would be progeny sacrificed on the altar of his perfectionism.

He wondered if Marie would ever forgive him, or if he'd ever forgive himself.

"Let her go," he managed in a voice that sounded strangely hoarse and ragged to his own ears. "Just let her go. Put her on a fucking plane and I'll recreate everything I can for you. All the experiments—everything."

"Are you sure?" the man asked. "Because I have an additional incentive for you."

Mason tilted his head so that he could see who he was speaking with. The speaker had the expected look of the Carnetti crime syndicate family, expensive suit, long blue-black hair tied back in a ponytail, and a prominent nose.

The man stooped so that Mason could see the image on his smart phone. It was a video of Colin.

"Daddy!" Colin was saying with his usual buoyant eagerness. "The man said if you help them I can see you!"

Mason's mind reeled with desperation. Somehow they had gotten Colin, left in his mother-in-law's care while he and Marie went on holiday. He was sure she would have sacrificed herself for Colin without question, trying to prevent an abduction.

That meant she was probably dead.

"That was before," the tall man said, his voice silky smooth with no small degree of satisfaction. "I call this after."

It was Colin again. He seemed to be sleeping. One side of his head was bandaged. Someone standing just out of range of the camera suddenly shoved a latex covered hand in front of the camera.

In it was a human ear, a small one. A child's.

Mason's body went into overdrive trying to break his bonds. The Carnetti stooge laughed shortly, watching him struggle.

"Like an exotic fish that somehow escaped its tank," he noted dryly, "finding out the hard way it has no power in its new environment. Go on and thrash all you like, little fishy. And when you tire of it, we will talk."

***

The overhead lights were ghastly, giving everything in the room a sickly greenish hue. The Carnetti goons had untrussed him. It took an update that Marie had been sedated to undergo her second surgery and some shots from a live feed into the surgical suite to convince Mason to cooperate.

They were going for her appendix this time, he was told. But they might leave it in if he came up with enough information before the operation began.

Mason could taste blood in his mouth. He'd been biting the inside of his cheek, a nervous habit he'd had since childhood.

"Water," he said, wondering how long he'd been there. Then wondered where there even was. He thought they were still in Italy. Usually, he had an excellent sense of time. He guessed maybe 12 hours had passed since he and Marie had retired to their rented villa for the night, the moonlight pouring into their room as they made love. He remembered her sleepy, satisfied smile as they drifted off to sleep, having enjoyed a vintage bottle of pinot noir provided by the management.

He sipped the bottled water slowly. He noted with a slight sense of surprise that it was in a glass bottle. Immediately, he envisioned himself smashing it against the hard surface of the conference table and slitting the throat of the man on the opposite side of the polished wood with the broken edges.

But he thought of Marie, and merely finished the water off before setting it back down.

He saw that he was being filmed. Cameras were set up in several locations, he wasn't sure which ones were on. Another dark-haired man in a suit removed his water bottle and replaced it with a microphone, taped to make sure that it was on.

The gray-haired man sitting opposite nodded at him and winked. He could have been anyone's kindly grandfather, Mason thought. Unless you read the papers. This man was a modern day Godfather involved in human trafficking, drugs, terrorism, and the theft of state secrets. This man, Aldous Carnetti, was rumored to have murdered his own mother so that he could marry his younger sister.

This man was beyond any boundaries of conscience or morality, and he wanted information on the Haploid Project.

"I thought we could begin," the gray-haired man said quietly into his own microphone, "With the correct name of the project."

Mason took a deep steadying breath so his voice wouldn't shake. He noticed that the monitor behind Aldous Carnetti was a live feed from the operating theatre. He recognized Marie lying motionless on a surgical table, her auburn hair covered with a sterile paper cap, her pale arms lying quietly at the side of the hospital gown she was wearing.

She seemed for the moment to be alone, in a curtained area.

He lowered his eyes to look into those of his captor.

"The official name is, The Replicant Security Initiative," he answered, leaning toward the microphone.

He paused, sweating. His thoughts were frantic.

"Go on," Aldous purred into his microphone. "What was your hypothesis? What prompted the research? Other than the greed of your corporate government, I mean."

Mason couldn't stop himself from glancing up at the monitor with Marie's image again.

"Well it was a silly idea, really," he said, slipping into the same mode he used when explaining the project to investment groups. "My son's hamster became ill. He was afraid that Barney—his hamster—was going to die. At the time I was working exclusively with mealworms and lower strata of life. My first impulse was to ask my wife to take the rodent to the vet—but then something made me hesitate. And I told Colin, my son…"

His voice trailed off as a jolt of pure rage coursed through him. Yes, his son Colin. The one that they had maimed, cutting off his ear… it was difficult to keep going as the image of the latex glove holding Colin's ear flashed in his mind.

"…to leave Barney with me," he forced out finally. "I had been experimenting with Haploid cells for some time, noticing that they had unique qualities that other human cells didn't. Under the right circumstances, they were far more active. I wasn't sure what the mechanism was…it was very early in the research at that point…"

A dark haired man about the same age as Aldous sitting several seats down on the same side of the table raised his hand and leaned forward into his microphone. Mason stopped speaking to listen.

"Haploids are only found in human reproductive cells," the man said. His voice was rough, guttural. "However, in the case of a worker bee they can spawn an entire organism. What made you think of this as something with advanced applications?"

"I didn't," Mason answered, "Not at first."

As the prepared train of speech continued, Mason's thoughts were racing. He had decided at some point to lie to his inquisitors as much as possible, while still giving plausible information.

And that presented a conundrum. At what point could he shift gears? Everything he'd told them so far was the gospel truth. It wouldn't take much more than this to place his forced dissertation into the traitorous category.

"I was actually intrigued by the C-value paradox," he went on, attempting to veer off into something that sounded clever and groundbreaking, but was essentially meaningless. "There were a lot of confusing *facts* floating around in the scientific community. Eukaryotic cells have two to ten times as many genes as prokaryotes—just that fact was counterintuitive. So I found myself asking why?"

Score! Mason's inner critic congratulated himself. You could hear a pin drop in the room. Several of the gentlemen around the table were scribbling notes. He definitely had their attention.

But for how long? Glancing back up at Marie's still body on the monitor he continued.

"This, along with the fact that they have many orders of magnitude more DNA in the cell indicated to me that we were missing something—some kind of key—some sort of Cyclin-based accelerant…"

A younger man wearing a pair of tortoiseshell glasses, sitting at the far end of the table leaned forward for the first time.

"Bull-fucking shit," he said pleasantly into the microphone. "Cyclin *also* halts production of the pre-replicative complexes. Now try again, Dr. Webb, and speak quickly. We are sending the surgeons in to remove Marie's appendix. They'll be painting her with Betadine now."

Cursing himself, Mason couldn't help but stare at the monitor which showed two masked and gowned individuals approaching Marie from two sides. Looking steadily up at the camera, one lowered the surgical blanket over the lower part of her bandaged body, past the apex of her thighs. He removed one glove and tossed it up on Marie's chest. As Mason and the men in the room with him watched he then held up his thick middle finger to the camera for a few seconds and then, still staring up at the camera, shoved the finger in between Marie's thighs, moving it back and forth rapidly.

One of the men at the conference table rumbled with laughter. Mason tried to stand, but was forced back down in his chair by two men who'd been standing behind him.

As he stared wildly across the table, Aldous said.

"Relax. They are just having a little fun with her, letting off steam before they open her up again," he said with a smile. "And you were doing so well, Mason, to a point. Your little son is just coming out of the anesthetic, vomiting a little. He should be fine though…with your help."

Mason cleared his throat, his heart thrumming in his chest.

"Stop hurting my family," he said into the microphone, his voice bouncing off the walls, the raw ache in it embarrassingly apparent.

"We hear you," the guy in the tortoiseshell glasses said smugly. "Power differential is a matter of perspective, right Mr. Webb? I for one am shaking in my booties."

Mason's head felt as if it were coming off.

"We know that the amount of DNA per genome has a null correlation with the presumed complexity of a species, as well as the amount of the DNA not correlated with the number of chromosomes."

"And the paradox? In layman's terms?" the man with the spectacles asked.

"The paradox is that the amount of DNA in the haploid cell of any organism is not at all related to its evolutionary complexity," Mason finished.

The bespectacled man snorted.

"Any idiot can Google that. Give me some original research, Dr. Webb. Your wife's surgery is about to begin."

Once again Mason's eyes drifted upward. There were four figures in the operating theatre now. One was obviously a nurse monitoring Marie's breathing, heartbeat, and blood pressure.

Suddenly another television monitor on the opposite side of the room flickered to life. He could hear his son's voice.

"Ow," Mason heard Colin say, turning his head from side to side in his state of stupor.

"Oooooow."

Panic had a taste, the dispassionate observer in Mason noted wryly. It was metallic, and acrid like vomit. Before he had another thought his mouth opened.

"We're talking recombinant DNA here," he said. "Not a secret in the scientific community, true, but what I discovered sent cell reproduction into overdrive. It made the difference and gave us the control we needed to design an organism to *exact* specifications. Refining the research gave us the ability to decrypt and preorder genes, tell them what to do, what to create."

"We're aware. We want specifics," the gray-haired man said quietly.

He shoved a tablet across the table at Mason.

"We start in six hours. You will recreate your work." he said. "Catalogue everything you need. Everything."

Mason noted his hands were shaking, but still he looked up at Aldous.

"I have to see my son," he said.

***

During torture sessions, Mason had found that he preferred it when the cartel goons beat him one after another. It was easier, because he became numb to their blows after the first two men had worked him over.

At one point in time he was fed and allowed to shower. Two hours of sleep were allowed to keep him functional. He couldn't tell if he was being tortured to assure his cooperation or because they thought he was lying to them, holding something back.

He was. And he intended to keep doing it to the best of his ability.

He had had one triumph. His request to see Colin had been granted. They had shackled him and led him down the hallway from the meeting room and around the corner to another long hallway. At the end of it was a sign marked "Infirmary" and it was there he saw Colin through a small glass window reinforced with metal gridding, still stirring in his sleep.

He ached to touch Colin. His rage rose up again and he shoved it back, certain he would harness that dark energy at some point, and not wanting to waste it.

They told him that Marie had a successful second surgery to remove her perfectly healthy appendix. Mason asked to see her also, but was denied. He hadn't even seen her on a monitor for six hours at that point, causing him to wonder if she were even alive. It was then he came to a realization.

Even if he could figure a way out, he couldn't save them both. He knew what Marie would say, of course. There was no sacrifice she wouldn't have made to keep their boy alive.

Grief had a flavor too, but he refused to taste it yet.

He would have plenty of time to regurgitate it later.

He had an opportunity to bathe again. They'd set up the lab and wanted him to dress properly, including wearing a lab coat.

It was when he was toweling himself off that he looked down and made a discovery that caused him a sharp intake of breath.

His scar was gone. The one that he'd had since childhood, when he and his parents had been involved in a horrific car accident and his ruptured spleen had had to be removed. It was a long scar starting several inches above his navel and ending several inches below.

It had faded over the years, but now it was completely gone.

His mind raced as it attempted to argue him out of the only conclusion he could make based on logic and deduction.

They called him Mason, but this body was not him.

The real Mason, the one the corporate government could not risk losing, the one that had been rejected time and again for requests to go on a holiday with his wife to a foreign country, was nowhere *near* this covert facility owned by the Carnetti Cartel.

He was here, because he was a replicant. He was a clone the original Mason *knew*, a final field test to unequivocally prove Mason's lifetime of research.

What an asshole.

He wouldn't risk having the information replicated. Even if he were able to recreate the Haploid experiments to the best of his ability, he doubted he could.

Was Marie a replicant also? No. Mason trusted her to discover if there were any fault in the replicant, and no one had anticipated the abduction.

And with that, he knew exactly what he was to do.

***

The lab was impressive. The energy was frenetic around Mason as he walked into the tricked-out facility. He knew this was the one window of time in which the power differential would shift in his favor, because in giving him this environment they had granted him a foothold in their world.

"Where are the cytoblasts?" he asked, as he did a walkthrough.

He had to admit, his captors had faithfully recreated a functional lab, following his specifications almost to the letter.

Those details could save him.

Mason began with a discussion of critical temperature considerations, citing a range for all the tissue and cytoplasts used.

Checking and rechecking slides of the 10 recombinant samples, Mason played the showman. He offered to replicate cells from one of the guards, and took a swab of the inside of the man's cheek to get a DNA sample. As time went on, the atmosphere became more relaxed. Mason had several scientists looking on through a glass partition. Some of the onlookers brought in extra seats far beyond the scientific stage so that they would not interfere.

Mason prepared different slides with different tints, knowing half his audience wouldn't understand what he was showing them. All the while he watched for a moment he was sure would come.

After three hours he felt the first tissue samples, which he had irradiated but had not treated with the enzyme cocktail that had been a part of the original Haploid Project, showed enough cell division to be impressive, and began inviting the scientists and others to look through the high powered microscopes and be amazed.

His performance was a true union of science and magic.

At that point the guard in the corner, the one with the machine gun, let it hang around his shoulder and stretched.

Mason crooked his finger at him and made a sweeping gesture, inviting him to take a look.

The guard walked over. Laughing and talking hid the whirring sound of an imbalanced centrifuge as it spun toward a climax. Mason ducked behind the guard as the unit exploded, sending shards of metal into every corner of the room and causing a shockwave that shattered the glass partition. He relieved the bleeding guard of his weapon. His operating knowledge of semiautomatic weapons was sketchy, but it was all he needed. He leaped through the newly opened window as everyone else reeled from the impact of the explosion.

A spray of machine gun fire into the gathering of well-dressed men shattered Aldous's jaw, causing it to separate and fall to one side of his astonished face.

Running through the back door and down the long hallway, he shot down the two sentries outside of the room marked *Infirmary*, then shot the young nurse with doe eyes who had been sitting in an armchair near Colin's bed, reading to him.

Colin was awake. His shocked eyes found and recognized Mason, and he flew to him, climbing up and clinging to him like a monkey.

He had expected guards outside the doors as he left, but saw none. The street was noisy with activity, colorful costumes, dancing, and a brass band. Of course. It was Carnival. He and Marie had traveled here for the festival. As an afterthought, Mason threw down the rifle and shucked off his blood-spattered lab coat, leaving them on the front porch. He cradled the son who still hugged tight to his neck and walked off, blending into the crowd.

***

The boy was nearly a teenager, now. He reached down to pick up a pebble as they walked and, drawing his arm back, pitched it into the ocean. He wore his sun-streaked blonde hair to his chin.

He was self-conscious about the missing ear, but he had a golden ring pierced through the other, and the rough hands of a fisherman's son. He seemed to look more like him every day, two beings cut from the same cloth.

The village was a remote one, and not a popular stop because the winds were rough, storms frequent, and the rocky shoals discouraged tourists.

Mason thought it was perfect. Quiet. He stayed away from the *grid*. Sometimes he wondered about the original Mason, whether he mourned his son and wife, or what he would have done if he'd been in his shoes.

But not too often.

He owed nothing to that life, and nothing to the man who forced him to make such terrible choices.

131

The Opal Ring

Elizabeth Alsobrooks

Jasmine accepted the white dove from her father's outstretched hand, smiled and gestured toward his gold-turbaned, bowed head as the gathering tourists clapped in appreciation. The marketplace was crowded for midweek, especially during the slow season. She was glad her father insisted they do a quick performance to generate additional interest for tonight's show. Hotel bookings were climbing again, but that didn't guarantee a full house with so many other entertainment choices available in Cairo. The talent scout was coming tonight. He had to believe her father could pack in the guests if they were going to get the Vegas contract. It was her father's lifelong dream, and she would do anything to get back to America and away from Uncle Hassam.

Jasmine slipped the dove into his cage, picked up the three rings and handed them to her father with a grand, graceful gesture, and smiled at the crowd before backing away. She had become quite a dutiful magician's assistant since they moved to her uncle's hotel after her mother's death six years ago. Her uncle was still working on transforming the American-born teenager into a subservient Egyptian female in his male-dominated household. He might have had better luck if she didn't have such clear and fond memories of a loving, independent American mother, and a father who adored and cherished her, and still mourned her passing. She knew about the locket with her mother's photo that he kept in his pocket and took out to gaze upon at odd moments, when he thought himself in solitude. It had his photo too. She knew because she had gifted it to her mother for her birthday the year before she died in that terrible automobile accident.

Glancing down, she moved her hand from her left wrist where she had been absently rubbing at the thin, vertical scar, now hidden by a permanent henna-hued tattoo of a Siamese cat trailed by little kitty paw-prints, the sun above its head dissected by a pentagram. "Sheba," she whispered, feeling the silky brush against her ankle, thankful for being pulled back to her duties by her faithful companion.

Since only she could see her, the cloaking spell Jasmine used as added protection for her beloved feline assured Sheba's access to even the most secure locations whenever needed.

She reached for the rings, gestured toward her father, smiled, and walked through the crowd, holding out a small hat to receive expected courtesy tips, glad for once that she was wearing the face veil if not the rest of the tourist expectation of a sexy belly-dancer.

It wasn't just her uncle's ass-grabs she had to worry about now that he'd convinced her father he'd boost his sales if she dressed like an Arabian magic show assistant to go along with his traditional magician garb. Her *costume,* graciously provided by her uncle*,* was little more than a skimpy bikini with transparent slit chiffon over her legs and arms, and a matching chiffon veil for her face and head. If only she could transport herself into a bottle to hide once in a while. She had to get away and soon, or it would be too late.

"That went well, don't you think?" her father asked.

"I was surprised at how many were here today," she said, handing her father the money.

"No, you keep it, Jasmine. I have more for you, too. You'll be needing some things for our trip to America." He laughed then, and Jasmine joined him, feeling an odd flicker of hope wriggle against the steel wall she had built around her heart six years ago. She hadn't seen her father's smile reach his eyes since her mother's death.

∞

"A wonderful act. Certainly grand and attention-grabbing. I'm not quite sure about the finale though. Something more over the top is necessary to sustain the crowds in Las Vegas. They're fickle and have such a diverse range to choose from. I'll be able to swing back in four weeks. Let's see if you can come up with a show-stopping final act by then. How's that?"

"Fair enough," her father told the scout.

Jasmine, eavesdropping from behind a set screen, couldn't help the slight drop in her shoulders as she let out her breath. It wasn't a crushing blow, but it was a disappointment. They had both hoped the man would offer her father a contract on the spot. Still, he had promised to come back again, a return visit in just four weeks, and tourist season would be high then. She mustn't give up.

Sheba had taught her that. Shortly after her thirteenth birthday when she was missing her mother and feeling particularly alone, Sheba, a tiny, bedraggled stray kitten had adopted Jasmine and on that same day continued to rub her little head against an old trunk until a small drawer popped open as though the feline had purposely revealed the secret compartment. Jasmine discovered her mother's *Book of Shadows* hidden in the old costume trunk. With it, she learned to enhance her father's magic with her own, just as her mother had done. It had encouraged him to focus on his magic again and turn less often to the bottle and other means of numbing his pain of loss.

She left the stage and slipped into the service hallway so her father wouldn't have to face her until he'd had time to compose himself. Despite his polite response, she'd noted the disappointment in his voice. He hadn't touched any alcohol or opium in over a year, and had promised Jasmine he was done with it for good. She knew he was trying. He was spending more time with her, becoming more like the father she remembered from her childhood before her mother's death. His magic continued to improve, too.

Her father was a fine magician, but with the aid of true magic, he performed feats that slight-of-hand entertainers could only mimic. She thought her power strong enough, but clearly she was wrong. To secure Vegas and escape her uncle, she must take no more chances. She needed to go speak with Ahmed, the hotel security assistant and Jasmine's best friend since she was an orphaned little girl in a strange land and he a scared new houseboy in a large casino hotel.

"What has you so distracted, little mouse?"

Jasmine froze. She refused to look up past the gleaming brown alligator loafers blocking her way. What was her uncle doing here? She took this hall to avoid him. Why hadn't she smelled that cloying musk he always wore? She stood in the shower for an hour to rid herself of its memory whenever he touched her.

"Kitty got your tongue?"

"What do you want?"

"Respect. We can start there. I gave you and your father a home when he lost everything to grief and a bottle. And worse. Do you remember that?"

"I remember everything." She looked up at him with defiance then, fueled by anger and undisguised hatred.

"That American arrogance. It's going to get you in over your head yet, little miss," he said, reaching out to grab her shoulders.

"Take your hands off me!"

He shook her like a bobble-head doll, until her neck felt like it might snap. Then his meaty hand slapped her face so hard her head bounced off the wall. Her neck hurt. It felt sprained. Her head throbbed. She blinked, trying to focus her vision, her attention.

"S-stop."

And then he was smashing his wet, drooling mouth against hers. She tried to pull her mouth away, tried to suck in air, to breathe, to survive. He grabbed her ass, his fingers brutal and bruising, jamming her against him, lifting her up so he could grind up and down against her crotch.

He turned, carrying her with him and slammed her back into the wall, wedging her there with his body weight, freeing his hands to mash her breasts. She jerked her head to the side, causing a spasm of pain to shoot down her back from the kink the twist put in her neck, and she gasped and gulped in air.

He raised his head and snarled through a vapor of stale cigar breath, "You need to learn your place. You will respect your elders and do exactly as you are told. Do you understand me?"

"No, leave me alone," she managed to rasp out in a broken whisper.

He squeezed, hard, crushing handfuls of tender flesh beneath his brutal domination. "I said, do you understand me?"

"I understand that you're a monster. Let me go!"

His attention focused on her nipples and he squeezed, twisting them until she cried out in agony, sure he would rip them from her body, "Please, no, stop, let me go."

He loosened his hold and then began to caress her breasts, still aching from his savagery. "That's better. You see. It can be nice or it can be not nice. It's entirely up to you. All you have to do is learn to be respectful."

"Please, just let me go," she pleaded, hating him for what felt like a lifetime of vulnerability, humiliation and helplessness. If only she were stronger, or her mother had lived long enough to teach her more. She needed that talisman! Her magic made her feel stronger. It gave her the confidence she needed to overcome her immobilizing fear of him, but she wasn't strong enough to escape and prevent him from sending his network of thugs in pursuit of them. Not yet. If her father got a job in America, he wouldn't dare interfere, and by the time he realized the move was permanent it would be too late for him to prevent it.

To her surprise, he lowered her to her feet and said, "For now. Think about what I said." Then he turned and walked away. Trembling, she rubbed the lump on her head. Feeling dampness she pulled her fingers down and saw that they were red with blood. "Damn you, Uncle Hassam. One day you will pay for this," she murmured. "I promise you." Unfortunately she knew why he had let her go. He enjoyed toying with her. He enjoyed feeding her fear, the continued torture of escalating her horrified anticipation of what was to come.

He'd been doing it for six long, endless, agonizing years, since she was twelve and first came to live with him in his foreign land with his unfamiliar customs and rules and foods and laws. She was terrified the first time her uncle put his hand under her dress and caressed her over her underwear, holding her in place when she tried to move away. The first time had been brief. Over so quickly she was confused. But later, he had held onto her and continued his fondling despite her protests, scolding her until he was finished, on his terms. And she had let him, in the end, too frightened and confused by his foreign language and rage.

At first she had complained to a loving but distracted father, who tried to listen but smelled strongly of alcohol and some other pungent smoke she didn't recognize as tobacco but understood made him sleep and forget his pain for a spell until he woke up and then spent more time with her mother's photo and his magic tricks than a daughter who had her mother's eyes and hair and smile, and who had a nanny and tutors and maids and servants to look after her. But everyone who looked after her had been so appalled, so aghast, and so affronted. In the end, she had been made to feel ashamed, mistaken, ungrateful, disloyal, and wrong.

Then, as she grew a little older, he grew bolder. He drew her across his knees, and pulled down her underwear and spanked her, hard, for any imagined infraction, when she was well past the age of being spanked, holding her in place, despite her protests. His hands punished, then lingered and caressed and wandered and offended, and terrified her tender young flesh.

That's when she finally complained to her father again, but again everyone was appalled, so aghast, affronted, she must have misunderstood. If only her mother had lived, had been able to explain such things to her. Yes, Jasmine had agreed, if only then.

The housemaid found her just in the nick of time they said, and it was a wonder her head hadn't sank below the water line in the bloody bath. All Jasmine really cared about was the fact that it seemed to keep her uncle under control for a while, at least until recently. She rubbed the henna-hued tattoo on her wrist and stumbled down the hallway, the opposite direction from the man she hated most in the world. He had made his intentions clear enough. Yes, it would be too late to escape his total domination of her body very soon. Very soon indeed.

∞

"You're sure it's the one from the scroll I've been studying?" Jasmine asked.

"It must be. I've never seen anything like it," Ahmed said softly.

"But why would it just be for sale like that, like a trinket? Oh, if only it *could* be true, right now when I need it most, Ahmed."

"It's the right era, the right design. The crazy merchant can't know what it is, I tell you."

"It's got to be a knockoff," Jasmine insisted. "Do you know how many cultists would kill to get their hands on this piece? It's been missing for centuries. We have to make sure that he never figures out he ever had anything more than a knockoff if it is the real thing." Feeling a sudden premonition that she was being watched, Jasmine looked around the narrow, crowded street of the marketplace. A few Bedouin in brightly colored robes were leading camels down the street a few shops ahead of them, while a vendor to her right shook a broom at ragged street urchins who had kicked an empty can too close to his display of Persian carpets. The rich aroma of freshly brewed Turkish espresso wafted on the afternoon air and combined with the scents of exotic spices, florals and tobaccos.

Ahmed turned and raised his head. "Let's grab something to eat before we head back, too. I haven't eaten yet and I smell fresh goat meat."

"How can you think of food at a time like this? You are always hungry."

"Okay, sorry. Come on. It's going to be fine. What have you got to lose?"

"My entire life savings, and the last chance I have to escape that monster, that's what," Jasmine snapped.

"I'm sorry. I didn't mean to make light of it. I was trying to ease your mood. I know how important it is. I would do anything to get you away from him. I'll do whatever it takes, you know that."

"Well, let's go see." Jasmine pulled the hood further over her face and darted into the so-called antiquities shop, known for its touristy knockoffs.

The two co-conspirators noted the proprietor, a portly Arab in colorful garb descending upon them with eager salesman demeanor, and browsed random artifacts, with feigned disinterest.

"Ah, would you like to buy a lovely necklace to grace the swan-like throat of your beautiful maiden companion, my good man? This very day I have acquired a necklace worn by Cleopatra herself, a gift from Marc Anthony. Or perhaps you would prefer a brooch, a jeweled scarab to bring you good luck."

"Just looking. Thank you. I don't wear much jewelry. Maybe a paperweight?"

"Oh! Such beautiful paperweights! Statues of Isis, Anubis, Osiris, the pyramids, come, see what all we have, right this way!" he said, gesturing toward the back of the store.

Jasmine dutifully followed, examining a few of the items he suggested, shaking her head and setting each one back down as if it wasn't what she sought.

Ahmed, an aisle away, held up the ring they had come seeking and said casually, "This is different. I don't suppose you like this?"

"What is it?" she asked, walking over to look at it.

The merchant followed, eager for a sale. "Oh, we just got that in a few days ago. An antiquity, from a long lost pyramid, the dealer assured me. A magic ring. See how it shines," he said, holding it up to the light.

Jasmine reached for it. "Oh, I don't know. It's an opal, isn't it? And I think it's a fire opal, too. Aren't they a soft stone, easily broken."

"No, no! Very strong. A gemstone. See how they have carved a pretty star shape into it? Can they do that with a soft stone? No! Very rare! It belonged to a god! A Pharaoh!"

"Close," Ahmed muttered softly.

Jasmine kicked him behind the merchant's back. "I don't know. How much? U.S. Dollars of course."

"U.S.?" She could practically see the dollar signs blinking behind his greedy little eyeballs. "Very rare. No less than $1000.00"

In Arabic Ahmed said, "$100.00 take it or leave it. We know it's a knockoff."

"$200."

"$150."

"$175."

"Sold," said Ahmed.

Jasmine handed the merchant the incredibly small amount of money and they left the shop with a priceless ancient gold and pentagram carved opal ring that legend had it once belonged to King Solomon, brought to him as a gift from God by the Archangel Michael himself. Legend also claimed that this fire opal held within its fiery depth power over the fiercest jinni the world had ever known and the wearer of the ring could command the magical jinni to do their bidding.

∞

"I don't know what has come over me lately, Jasmine, but I feel like I can perform even the most difficult feats flawlessly, like when your mother was alive. I want to practice the tiger act today. When the scout comes tomorrow, I want to perform it. I think it will assure me that Vegas contract," her father said.

"I think you're right," she agreed, smiling. She saw Ahmed's look of concern and turned away. It was all worth it and everything was turning out better than she could have wished for. Nothing in life was free. If she had to give away all her jewels what did she care? She still had a beautiful opal ring, and it was all the jewelry she would ever need. Just let her uncle try to come near her now.

She hurried around backstage, putting the equipment away. As she sprinkled some birdseed into the dove cage feeder, Ahmed said, "What happens when you don't have any jewelry left?"

Jasmine glanced up and said, "I thought you were working the night shift. Don't worry so much. I just buy more, silly."

"I swapped with Mullah, and I'm worried about you. That's what friends do. So what if you don't have enough money to buy enough jewels? What then? Have you thought of that? I think we might have made a mistake." His brow creased with concern and the usual sparkle in his golden eyes was darkened by worry. "Don't use the ring again, Jasmine. Please. Give it to me and let me sell it. I can get more than enough money to buy tickets to America."

"No. My father won't just leave. He has to get this job. I can't leave him here. Uncle Hassam will turn him back into an addict in no time. He has no idea how evil his brother is. Uncle Hassam is nothing but friendly and solicitous in front of father. He sees his offer to handle all our business affairs from the hiring of my tutors and nannies to father's tailor as a family kindness, not the controlling and manipulative act it is. I'll manage somehow. I will. I must!" Jasmine set down the feed and turned to Ahmed.

She looked down at the ring that seemed to dwarf her hand and felt suddenly heavy. Cupping her right hand in her left as though to support it, she looked him in the eye. "He's doing so well now. It-it would destroy him. Please. Pl-ease. You said you would do anything. Did you mean it? Then support me in my decision, Ahmed. I don't have any other choice. Time has run out. The scout comes tomorrow. What if he turns father down again? Would you prefer that we kill my uncle to get my father away from the evil that surrounds him? To get me away from my uncle's evil intentions?"

"When I think of--"

"Ahmed! You promised not to do anything rash." She grabbed his clenched fist and drew it to her chest until he relaxed his grip.

"No. No, of course not," he said with resignation.

"Then please just support me in this. I am under enough strain. Come help me get the tigers ready, since you're here. My father wants to practice for tomorrow's show."

"I didn't mean to add to your burden. I would never do that," he said quickly, raising his hand to tuck a curl behind her ear, then dropping his hand and looking away in sudden embarrassment. "I'm happy to help you. You know I listen to too many of auntie's stories. This one chore, I actually love. The tigers are beautiful, but fearsome."

Jasmine turned back to her task to hide the flush in her cheeks. "Remember that. They are dangerous, no matter how gorgeous. Wild animals are never fully tame," she said softly, putting the feed away and heading down the corridor toward the back courtyard that housed the tiger cages.

"No, you remember that, Jasmine. Wild creatures are not to be trusted, especially Jinn!"

"Shhh. Do you want someone to hear you?" she whispered as they turned the corner and Ahmed opened the courtyard door.

The handlers and tiger trainers were already there when they arrived, grooming and caring for the beautiful beasts. They were huge, eight in all, the largest one well over five-hundred pounds. Though they were kept constantly clean and their straw freshly forked, there was no mistaking the animal scent wafting through the warm courtyard. The group had been together for several years and chuffed and roared, communicating with one another, knowing their pack ranking, but like all wild animals testing their boundaries from time to time. Jasmine went up to the head trainer.

After greeting him with a warm smile, she said, "We intend to use all the tigers for the final act tomorrow, Rajah, so my father wants to practice it now. We'll be doing the swap as the finale, but he wants to do the levitation and appearance of all the tigers at once, with me floating in the air, center stage in place of Simba, above the revolving circles of fire."

"All at once? I'm not sure about that, Jasmine. How will we orchestrate that many cats? They aren't trained to stand stationary behind those little camouflage walls inside the cages for very long. The act would have to move pretty fast."

"Yes, we know. Don't worry. My father has it all under control. That's why we're going to do a practice drill today. Ahmed knows how it's supposed to be set up. He'll show you where the cages need to be. Can you help him get it ready while I go change my clothes?"

"Sure. We'll meet you on stage, Jasmine. If it works, it's going to be a great act."

"Oh, it'll work, and it's going to be a fantastic act," she agreed.

With a quick wave, Jasmine headed toward the service hallway and her rooms. She needed to be certain that Ornias, the jinni of the Ring, was ready to perform *his* magic. Glancing down, she noticed that she was rubbing her thumb across the henna-hued tattoo on her wrist and dropped her hand to her side, hastening her departure. A movement in the hallway from the right caught her eye and she smiled. "Sheba," she said softly. "It won't be long now, my precious little familiar."

Reaching the elevator, she entered, slipped in her key card, hit the 4th floor button, and stepped back. The car moved up smoothly and silently, the doors swooshing open with a soft chime. She stepped out to the right until habit brought her to the third door where she used her pass key to enter her room. Sheba brushed against her leg to hurry past her, knowing her dinner was already waiting in the pantry.

Jasmine picked up the remote, downed the blinds, upped the lights, and locked the doors. She grabbed a bottle of water from the small fridge in the bar area, took a swig, and set it down. Her thumb found its way to the thin vertical scar on her wrist. Ahmed had been helping her search for an artifact such as this ring for almost two years. Only a few magic-bearing items would have given her the potential magic she needed to boost her own power enough to escape the insidious financial and filial ties her uncle held over them. Though they lived in the most likely place in all the world to find such a treasure, she still found it incredible that they had recovered the most powerful talisman of all, *The Opal Ring* of King Solomon. She would have been willing to steal it to get away from Uncle Hassam, but she was relieved that they had managed to buy it for such a small fee.

Ahmed had all but changed his mind right after they got back with their find. He had nearly convinced her that they could find another way, some way that wouldn't land him on the bottom of the Nile in the belly of a crocodile, with her chained in a private brothel cell where her father couldn't find her and her uncle would. In the end, her personal desperation made her less terrified of the unknown consequences.

They'd spent another week researching the use and significances of the ring, and she had prepared for its use, or so she assured Ahmed. Finally, casting a powerful protection spell within a guardian circle, Ahmed at her side, she had summoned the jinni, and he had as all the ancient scrolls had foretold appeared in a swirling pillar of fire. The jinni acknowledged her as his mistress, too, the bearer of the ring, but he was so frightening, so obviously powerful.

Despite the protection spells she had cast, Jasmine felt anxious with her new acquisition. This would be the second time she summoned the jinni. She knew what to expect, she told herself. Taking a deep breath, Jasmine rubbed the ring on the middle finger of her right hand. The air around her crackled and sparked, a pillar of fire shot from floor to ceiling, swirling like a tornado, scorching hot, with pain but no damage, like hell, and in a puff of black smoke it disappeared. In its place stood an eight foot jinni, Ornias, once enslaved by King Solomon to carve stones for the building of the temple. According to the mystic tomes, his enslavement was punishment for stealing gems from the royal treasury, gems he craved for their sparkling light. He would sink his vampire-like fangs into them and drain their glimmer in an effort to relieve the agony of eternal darkness—a life without the sun's blessing. This was the addiction Jasmine must feed in order to command the demonic jinni's magic.

She concluded that his explosive manner of reappearance was certainly that of an escaping addict and it in no way reassured her. The jinni was manlike in appearance, save that his skin was ebony not in an African ebony way, but more like a preternatural obsidian sheen with eyes that glowed golden like a cat's, but with a sunset luster that spoke of darker, more underground locales than mountaintops or beach horizons. "I hunger!" he bellowed.

Her own meager jewelry stash was nearly gone, so she had spent every penny she had left after purchasing the supposedly *fake* ring from the poor misguided antiquities dealer to buy loose gemstones in the marketplace. She handed a few of those to him now. He snatched them eagerly. Next, if need be, she would take her uncle's ruby tie tack, with no remorse whatsoever—but she wouldn't involve Ahmed in even the knowing of it. It would be her sin and her consequences alone. On her terms.

The creature held a small stone in his hand, and it grew to enormous proportions until she had to shield her eyes from the luster of its gleam. He smiled, a hideous distortion of happiness, and his incisors distended, enabling him to sink his teeth into the magically engorged stones. She watched in amazement as he appeared to suck the stone's shine until the blue topaz turned first gray and then black as coal. He repeated the process with first the small garnet and then the sapphire she had given him. Then, sated for the moment, he said, "Your wishes, mistress?"

"I wish to be protected, from my uncle. I wish also to have you aid my father's magic." She went on to explain the details of her plan.

∞

The audience was silent as the eight cages rose in the air. They hovered, shoulder-height to The Amazing Ben Ali as he stood center stage, arms raised. He walked to the cage closest to him and with a quick tug pulled the gold drape from the previously empty cage, revealing a full grown Bengal tiger. As if on cue, it roared to the accompanying gasps and ah's of the appreciative audience. Ben Ali hurried from cage to cage, releasing the drapery and revealing six more Bengal tigers. But when he came to the center cage, the one that had in fact already contained a tiger, what he revealed instead was Jasmine, smiling and waving. The cages slowly lowered to the floor, and The Amazing Ben Ali opened the cage to release Jasmine, who he led to center stage where they took a bow and turned to gesture toward the tigers.

When they stepped forward, the curtain came down behind them, allowing the handlers to hurry the tigers off stage and away from the wild applause that made the cats nervous and skittish, back to their larger cages, juicy meat treats and quiet praise from familiar voices. Jasmine bent her head one last time, gestured toward the true star, her father, and then graciously backed away, smiling with joy at her father's beaming pride.

The talent scout was waiting for them backstage once her father finished his second curtain call. He laughed when her father just shrugged and refused to divulge the levitation method used for the cages when the scout, a self-proclaimed amateur magician himself, was unable to find the wires. Despite his disappointment, the man produced the coveted contract, and Jasmine managed to keep from squealing with excitement as she hurried off to find Ahmed and allow her father to finish his business negotiations.

Once in the corridor, she noticed a burning sensation on the middle finger of her right hand. Looking down, she saw that the pentagram on the opal ring was glowing from within. It pulsed with radiant fire, sparks of blue and green, orange and gold twinkled up and down the lines of the symbol. She felt Sheba brushing against her legs, swishing her tail and winding in and out around her ankles as if she could feel the electrical impulses the ring was generating. The burning sensation increased and the gold began to glow with a rosy hue, almost molten. Jasmine grabbed hold of the ring and tried to pull it from her finger, but it wouldn't budge. Rushing into a nearby restroom, she turned on a faucet and plunged her hand under the cool water. It had no effect.

She rubbed against the ring, trying to ease it off her finger, and in so doing activated the stone. The room vibrated and a pillar of fire erupted from the floor to ceiling, then exploded into a puff of smoke and the jinni appeared.

The ring immediately stopped burning and returned to its natural state. "You did that! What are you doing?" Jasmine demanded.

"I hunger!" declared the jinni, clearly agitated.

"But I fed you just before the performance and I don't have any more gemstones right now. I told you I will get you more tomorrow. You said ruby and diamonds last the longest and I will get you some from my evil uncle tomorrow. I know where he keeps his. My father got his contract and everything is going to be okay now."

"I hunger!" shouted the jinni.

"Okay, okay." Jasmine pushed air with her hands, indicated that he should be quiet. She bent down and was surprised and relieved to see no one was in the bathroom. "I will get them now. He will be in the club for a few more hours, so no one will be in his rooms. Get back in the ring and I will get them for you now."

"As you command, mistress," the jinni said, and vanished.

Jasmine took a deep breath. Glancing in the mirror, she noted the smudged knoll under her left eye, and wet a paper hand towel to wipe at the smear. Then, splashing a bit of cool water on each flushed cheek, she dabbed them dry, dropped the towel in the trash can and pulled the door open, nearly colliding with a middle-aged tourist in a sequined gown, chatting into an International iPhone. Murmuring an apology, she turned right and hurried to the elevator.

By the time the elevator reached the 7th floor, she managed to get her breathing back to normal. As the door swooshed open, she stepped out and looked toward the end of the corridor, where her uncle occupied the last two rooms, having had them converted into one oversized suite, reserving the penthouse suites on the upper floors for up-charged guests while still living in more luxurious accommodations as the hotel's owner. He really was a greedy bastard, she reminded herself. A few less gems were certainly not going to hurt him, and he'd been underpaying her and her father for six years, not to mention the fact that he'd been molesting her since she was a twelve-year-old child. He had whatever she did coming to him, and then some, she reasoned.

Not that she had any choice, she reminded herself, as she paused at the storage room door and slid her pass key through the card reader. She stepped inside, found a box of latex gloves and wriggled her fingers into a pair, then hurried back into the hallway.

Soon she was swallowing her fear as she approached his door. Knocking, and then holding her breath in case he should actually be in for some bizarre twist of fate, Jasmine glanced back down the corridor. When no one responded, she pulled out the pass key she'd had forever, and shoved it in the card reader. The lights flashed green from left to right and back again. She heard the familiar click, and pressed down on the lever. The door opened, and she was in. Just like that.

Looking around, she was surprised at the décor in her uncle's suite. She wasn't sure what she had expected, but it was nothing like hers or her father's rooms, and nothing like the plush lobby or even the elegantly appointed dining room, casino or showroom where her father and some Arabian dancing girls performed. It was beautiful, but it was modern and it was designed with western European furnishings. She could have been standing in the lobby of a New York City loft on the Upper East Side, not the entrance to a Cairo hotel owner's suite. Where were the gilded ankhs and busts of Pharaohs and framed papyrus fragments? Surely he should have at least one statue of Isis or an Eye of Horus for good luck? He was such a hypocrite. The man did nothing but put her down for being an uppity American and yet he surrounded himself with Western everything.

Jasmine laughed at the irony, but had no time to wonder what further perversions her twisted uncle harbored. She hurried in the direction she felt would be his bedroom and sought out the closet.

How convenient of her uncle to use the same architect and designer for all the family suites. Though much grander than her small suite, the closet was similar. He was so predictable in some ways. Finding the remote, she picked it up right where he had left it, on top of his dresser in the middle of his closet, and pressed the button that opened his drawers. She found his jewel valet easily enough too, in the same general location as her own meager and now nearly empty small-cubby-partitioned drawer. Upon discovering far more gems than expected, she helped herself to a pair of diamond cufflinks as well as the large ruby tie tack she had seen him wear on several occasions, closed the drawers and ran toward the entry door.

She was out the door and waiting for the elevator before it dawned on her that she had just committed a burglary. In fact, she was now a jewel thief, a cat burglar. Perhaps she should teach Sheba to burgle. The jinni would have to make the security camera footage glitch her out of the appropriate time frames of course, and the pass card key code would have to be erased from the system on her uncle's door, but other than the electronic help from the jinni it had gone much easier than she could have wished.

An elderly couple exited the elevator, barely noticing her as she stepped inside and pushed the 4th floor button. What was one more Arabian dancing girl in Cairo? She had to get out of her costume. Remembering her gloves, she pulled them off and wadded them into a ball in her hand. The door chimed and she exited, thankful that no one was waiting to enter. She hurried to her rooms, shoved her key card into the reader and all but slammed it behind her, collapsing against it. Shaking, reaction catching up to her, she reached down to scoop up Sheba whose immediate response to her traumatic entrance served to soothe her. "Aw," she said softly, responding to the gentle purr and rubbing of the round head against her neck that her spiritual familiar offered by way of a tender snuggle. "Thanks, Sheba. I needed that."

Setting Sheba on the floor, she picked up the gloves where she had dropped them, walked over to toss them in the trash, and sighed. There was no delaying any longer. She knew what had to be done. Jasmine rubbed the ring and watched as the jinni appeared, eager to see what she had brought him. His golden eyes sparkled when he saw that she had a ruby as well as twin diamonds.

"You have done very well indeed, mistress. Ornias is grateful."

"Good. I need you to erase my image from the hotel video cameras and my hotel pass key code from my uncle's room card reader so they can't connect me with the disappearance of these gems. I probably should have told you that before I did it, but I'm not exactly a professional."

The jinni waved his hand in a casual manner and said, "It is done, mistress. A small matter."

"What spell did you use?" Jasmine asked, curiosity making her bold.

Ornias paused. He lowered the already enlarged ruby and bent forward to gaze at her intently. Grabbing her wrist, he turned it over and held it within his hand and studied the henna-hued likeness of Sheba, the sun-rendered pentagram, the little kitty paw prints, and then looked again, deep into her eyes, her soul, and said, "So, you are a witch who wishes to be a sorceress, it would seem. Why did you not just voice this wish aloud, mistress?"

"I-I. No one knows of this. I have never…"

"But I, Ornias, most powerful of all magic casters should have sensed this flicker of power secreted away within you, mistress. I was too consumed by my own addictions to notice what lurks in the hearts of those around me. I have been too long in solitude it would seem." Suddenly he shrank, becoming a *mere* six foot tall with mocha human skin tone, and strode over to Jasmine's closet, throwing open the door. He walked to the back and stood before her altar, observing her statue of Isis, her incense burner, her chest of herbs and apothecary spices and resins. "Upon King Solomon's death, I bound myself to this ring and hid it where I felt no one would ever find it. What I should have done is destroy it, this ring that had for so many years controlled me. I thought if I left this world, I would no longer suffer. Little did I realize that my hunger would only grow as I languished in this void, a prisoner of my own foolish whim. I see now that I must break my own spell."

He rummaged through her chest, pulling out what he sought, grinding some ingredients using her mortar and pestle. When he was done, he put out his hand and said, "The ring."

She hesitated, but didn't dare defy him, so handed him the ring. After all, he had already granted her wishes. The *coming true* part was under way, and she had paid the fee.

He placed the ring upon the altar, gestured toward it and it sparked and flamed. A softly chanted incantation in an ancient tongue she didn't recognize filled the small confines of her closet and the flickering flames from the fire cast strange shadows upon the walls, making her imagine she saw dancing creatures, bathed in flames, horns protruding from their foreheads. But in an instant they were gone, the flame had snuffed itself out, the incantation was over, and the jinni said, "Here, a pretty bauble now, but my prison no more," and handed her the ring.

She took it and slipped it back on her finger, silently, not sure what, if anything she should say. A knock on the door saved her the decision. The jinni disappeared, as if in agreement. Confused, Jasmine looked around her closet, which was now once again as she always kept it, the way her mother had taught her. She went into her bedroom and closed the door behind her, then went into the foyer to answer her door.

The peep hole revealed Ahmed, much to her relief, and she quickly opened the door.

"I heard you have good news for me!"

"If you already heard, it's not news," she said.

"I thought you'd be happier," he said, head tilted, studying her. "What's wrong?"

"Nothing."

"Ha! If there's one thing I've learned in life it's that whenever a female says that, the opposite is true. I have five sisters, remember? Give!"

Jasmine laughed without humor. "Okay. The jinni broke the spell and is no longer tied to the ring. I am no longer his mistress, but it doesn't matter because as you already know I was granted my wishes."

"Ah, is that all? Well, that's more good news if you ask me. That means we are now free of him. I was very worried. No good can ever come of messing with a jinni. They are dangerous. Even if you have them under a spell, unlike angels they have free will and so can be very, very evil and are powerful sorcerers, unrivaled in their casting of spells and curses."

"And just how do you know all this?" Jasmine demanded.

"My auntie was telling me the legend of--"

"Not more of your auntie's stories now, Ahmed. Come on. I have to shower and change. And I'm starving. How about I meet you for dinner in an hour so we can celebrate my father's new contract. I'm sure he has already gone out with the talent scout and his magician friends. We can go to the café in the square that you like so much. It's open late tonight."

"A plan I can work with. It'll give me time to go change. I didn't know we were going out. I will be downstairs in the lobby in one hour." With a quick wave, Ahmed was out the door.

∞

Jasmine reached up to touch her talisman, and stopped. Going back to her bathroom, she scanned the countertop, then retraced her route to her closet and looked through her jewelry valet, but couldn't find her necklace anywhere. She knew she'd been wearing it during tonight's performance. She always said a small protection spell her mother had taught her before going on stage. The cage. There had been a slight tug on her neck as she slipped into the hidden compartment in the bottom of the tiger cage in preparation for her miraculous *appearance* during the show's grand finale. The necklace must have fallen off. Perhaps she had snagged it on something and broken the clasp. It was a cherished gift from her mother. She had to find it. Grabbing her key card, Jasmine headed for the door. Ahmed wouldn't be waiting yet as she was ready twenty minutes early.

The elevator opened as soon as she pushed the button, and swooped straight to the ground floor. She quickly went to the big room off the courtyard where they housed the tigers and equipment overnight and let herself in with her key card. The cats, already settled for the evening, stirred at the unexpected intruder, but settled down once she spoke to them quietly. Hers was a familiar, calming voice.

She approached the stage cages and found the one with the markings she sought. Opening the door with a soft clanking noise, she stepped inside and lifted the trap door in the floor.

"Hey, little mouse. I saw you come in here. Come to play with the big kitties?"

She froze. Her uncle. He followed her. Quietly, she lowered herself into the small cubicle and closed the door, concealing herself as she had done so many times before. As she lowered her hand, it fell upon a cluster of stones. Her necklace. She clasped it tightly, repeating the protection spell in her head, over and over.

"Come out, come out, wherever you are, little mouse. There's only one way out."

His voice was close now. He sounded like he was right outside the cage. She closed her eyes and squeezed the talisman, wishing their positions were reversed.

Suddenly, she was standing outside the cage.

"Hey, what the hell just happened? Where am I?" shouted her uncle.

Pounding sounded on the underside of the trap door of the cage.

"Let me out of here!"

Jasmine stared, fascinated that her wish had come true. But then a Bengal tiger appeared in the cage, and then another. They roared, and it was a hungry sounding roar. Very hungry.

The trap door popped open.

Jasmine stared, transfixed in horrified fascination as her uncle's shouts of outrage became screams of agony until there was silence except for the rending and chomping and crunching and gnawing and slurping. And the gasping, of course, there was gasping and panting, but that was Jasmine, not the tigers. She was half-way to hyperventilating when the jinni appeared.

"Let your breath out slowly. Would you like a paper bag?"

She shook her head, and forced air from her lungs, then more air, then a little more. Then she allowed a bit to come back in. Then out. Her hands were clutching her throat and she loosened them. Once she could speak, she said, "I didn't wish this. Never this. Why couldn't my own magic have just worked?"

"Your own magic? But it did. Why do you think he never raped and tortured you, like the other girls in the hotel?"

"But he molested me!"

"Yes, he was a monster. And he did so much worse to so many. His fate is as it should be, but you had to be toughened up to fit the role for which you have been chosen. You are not asking the right questions."

"What? What role have I been chosen for? What questions should I ask?"

"You are not asking why King Solomon was given dominion over me."

"But I thought it was because you stole gems."

"Do you think for this reason alone the Archangel Michael would be sent to give King Solomon the means to control me?"

Jasmine gasped. It was a reasonable explanation, but when put like that, it did seem as though the crime may not fit the punishment. "Wh-what did you do?"

"I do not have these," he opened his mouth and displayed his fearsome incisors, causing her to back away a step, "just so that I can suck the light from gemstones." He appeared inside the cage. The tigers were now gone. Grasping what was left of her uncle, he drew him up and again opened his mouth. Sparks, blue, green, orange, yellow and purple twinkled along two continuous threads of cosmic plasma that pulsed from her uncle's corpse through the straw-like suction of the jinni's teeth into the jinni's essence. She knew this because once again his skin was translucent obsidian in appearance and she could see the same cosmic sparking burst throughout his being like a galaxy creation. Her uncle was pulp, puff, gone.

"S-soul sucker," Jasmine whispered, eyes wide with shock, body shaking like a forgotten thread yet to be woven into the tapestry of life.

"Very astute."

"What do you want of me?" she asked, dreading the answer.

"What I was promised," the jinni said. "What your mother promised and failed to deliver," he added. Then he vanished.

"My mother?"

She spun around, but the room was truly empty. Running to the door, she flung it open and ran to the elevator. A young man collided with her when the doors opened, and apologized, though it was clearly her fault. Jasmine nodded, distracted, and pushed the 4th floor button. Her father was probably out, but she had to be sure. The elevator took forever, stopping at every floor to let guests on or off. Tempering her impatience with difficulty, she finally got off and hurried to her father's rooms.

A knock on his door was answered almost immediately by a, "Come on in, I'm on the phone."

Thrilled to hear her father's voice, Jasmine hurried inside just as her father said, "Thanks, medium rare is perfect," and hung up.

"You didn't go out with the talent scout or your friends? Did something go wrong?" she asked, suddenly concerned about her father's contract deal, wondering if the jinni had done something.

"He had to catch a flight, and I had a slight headache, so made arrangements to celebrate with them tomorrow night. It's been a long weekend. The contract is all signed, sealed, and filed with my attorneys, so no worries there, my dear."

"Oh, good, about the contract. Congratulations, father. I knew you would get the deal. I'm sorry you're not feeling well though."

"Just a slight headache. Nothing at all, really. Took some aspirin and it's already on its way out."

"Great. How soon do we leave for America?" Not soon enough for her. She wanted to get away from Egypt and the jinni immediately. How long before they went looking for her uncle? He was such a pervert he sometimes disappeared for a few days at a time to some hellhole brothel, probably where he could do things depraved and illegal to underage street children no one ever missed. Cairo had enough of them, unfortunately. The jinni was probably right about that. Considering what her uncle was capable of, her magic probably had saved her from some even nastier horrors. But she had an unsettling suspicion that somehow the jinni or those who served him had *allowed* her uncle to abuse her in order to, how had he put it, *toughen her up*. Jasmine shuddered. It would be great if they could be gone before he was missed.

"Are you cold?"

"What? Oh, no. Just had a chill. Ever felt like someone walked over your grave type of thing?" Jasmine wrapped her arms around herself and rubbed her upper arms to dispel the goose flesh.

Her father's eyes transfixed with horror as he stared at her right hand. He reached out and pointed with his index finger.

"What is it?" she asked.

"That ring! Where did you get it?"

"This?" She grasped the opal ring and began to tug on it, twisting and turning, but it refused to move.

Her father grabbed her hand and pulled it until she finally cried out in protest. "We have to get it off," he said. "How did you find it? I flushed it down the commode on the jet before we landed six years ago!"

"What? What are you saying, father? You have seen this ring before?"

He backed away and ran his hand through his hair, looking haggard, older than his forty-eight years of a sudden. "It was your mother's. It was buried with her."

"Then how could you have had it on the plane? You're not making sense." *Her mother's? Had her mother been the jinni's last mistress?*

"You were too old for dolls, but you kept it with you because your mother had given it to you. I opened the window blind on the plane and the sunlight sparkled off the opal on the ring. It was around the doll's ponytail."

"So how do you know mother didn't put it there on the doll?"

"She couldn't do it anymore, couldn't stand being around those vile men, and couldn't see what that creature did to them. She tried to explain, tried to bargain with the jinni, but he wouldn't see reason. We were going to flee, find someone who could break the spell, but the very next day that car, it came out of nowhere." He wasn't focused on Jasmine any more, but seemed to be reliving the incident in his mind, the terror of it fresh on his face. "Do you really think it was just an accident?"

"What?" *Her beautiful sweet mother had fed the jinni souls? Sinful souls like her uncle's?* "The jinni killed momma?"

"She just couldn't make herself available to all those hideous, evil perverts any more, the kind of dark souls the jinni savors. She would never have led the jinni to her own beloved daughter. I saw the ring on her finger when I closed her casket myself!" He staggered back, clutching at his chest.

"Father!" Jasmine rushed forward, grabbing his arm. "What is it?"

"Just out of breath. Nothing," he said, gasping. But then his knees buckled, and he fell to the floor, doubled over in pain.

Jasmine grabbed the phone and called the front desk, demanding the house doctor and an ambulance. She hurried back to her father, whose face was blue, eyes open but staring straight ahead, and loosened his collar. "Father, can you hear me?"

The air crackled and a pillar of fire erupted from floor to ceiling, exploded into a swirl of smoke and the jinni appeared and said, "He doesn't look too good, does he?"

"Can you do something?" Jasmine sobbed.

"Can or will? Do you wish I would?" inquired the jinni, sounding almost sympathetic. "I'm really very hungry though," he added.

A knock sounded on the door and Jasmine yelled, "Come in, hurry!"

Ahmed raced into the room. "What's wrong? I heard the front desk call for a doctor and ambulance for your father's room!"

"Very," said the jinni again. "He looks tasty."

Ahmed stopped. He looked at the jinni, then back at Jasmine, crouched on the floor next to her father. "No. Wait! I'll get someone," he said, running from the room. A moment later, he was back, dragging the room service attendant with her father's dinner cart. "Look. Will he do?"

Jasmine stared at Omar, recalled him hiding behind the floor-to-ceiling drapes of an empty hotel suite, peering out while her uncle fondled and punished her naked flesh with blows that left bruises in both hidden and permanent places. The look on his face had not been sympathy, though the words he had expressed later were all the right ones, fearing retribution should her uncle discover his witness of the incestuous incident. Even so, could she hand his soul over to this demon, become every bit as monstrous as the jinni himself? She looked down at her father, then back at Omar, who fixated on the jinni in mute dread.

"Yes, why not him?" Jasmine said softly.

"Why not indeed," said the jinni. With a wave of Ornias' hand the young service attendant wreathed on the floor, clutching his chest. Within moments the heaving of his chest slowed and then stopped. The jinni approached. He reached down to grasp the young man's shirt front and lifted him from the carpet. When he opened his mouth, his incisors extended and the cosmic feeding frenzy Jasmine had previously witnessed was played out for Ahmed's horrified edification.

The service attendant disappeared within the jinni, who also vanished, and then Jasmine's father stirred and looked around. Sitting up, he said, "What happened?"

Indeed, thought Jasmine with a shudder, tears running unchecked down her face. She exchanged a bewildered look with Ahmed and said, "You passed out, father. The doctor and paramedics are on the way. I fear you may have had a stroke, or a heart episode of some kind."

"What? I'm too young for such things, surely. Funny I don't seem to recall anything past signing that contract this evening. There now, what's this? Don't cry, my little angel. I'm fine."

"You remember nothing?" Jasmine asked.

"No. Wait, is that my supper? I remember ordering supper. Starving too."

A knock sounded. "Finally. Come in!" Jasmine called out, wiping at her face and reaching for the tissue Ahmed held out to her. The doctor, followed closely by the paramedics with a stretcher arrived.

"I'm so sorry. I wasn't on the premises. Came back as soon as I got the call. What seems to be the problem?" the doctor asked.

Jasmine rose to her feet. "My father. He complained of a headache earlier. Then he had chest pains, passed out, turned blue, and he wasn't breathing well. He took aspirin. Seems better now, but he doesn't remember any of it, which worries me too," she said quickly before her father could tell the doctor nothing was wrong with him.

"Let's take a look," the doctor said, taking the stethoscope from his neck, putting the ends in his ears and placing it on her father's chest despite his protests. He placed his fingertips against her father's wrist and monitored his watch. Satisfied, he nodded and said. "We're going to take you in and run a couple tests. Best to be safe." Her father started to complain and the doctor added, "For your daughter's sake," which gained his begrudging cooperation.

"We'll be right behind you, father."

"Yes, not to worry. I will accompany Jasmine so the doctor may ride with you to hospital," Ahmed said.

"Thank you," Jasmine said. "I need to run to my room and get my purse. Then we'll be right behind you."

They waited until the paramedics had loaded her father onto the gurney and wheeled him into the hallway before rushing down the hall to Jasmine's room.

When they entered, she pushed the on lights button and rushed into the living room.

"He'll be fine, you know."

"Ah!" she cried out, jumping, startled to find the jinni seated casually waiting for her.

"You got what you wanted," Ahmed said, stepping in front of her, protectively, though she could see his hands shaking and hear the tremor in his voice. "Why are you here?"

"They will tell you he has had a mild stroke, the only side effect of which will be the memory loss. I'm afraid he won't remember the secrets you wish to know of his time with your mother either, though I'll not rob him of their love. That would be needlessly cruel. Don't you agree?"

"You have become one of the monsters you feast upon," Jasmine said softly. Then, more forcefully, "Did you kill my mother? Did you trick me into finding the ring?"

"What?" Ahmed said. "I thought your mother died in an auto accident, and I found the ring in that shop."

"So did I, until my father told me just now that it was the jinni who killed her, and that this ring belonged to her, first. Just how did it come to be there, in plain sight, just when you were at the antique store looking, and how did that dealer not know it for what it was?" Jasmine insisted.

"Your mother broke her end of the bargain," the jinni said, smiling without amusement. "But what of you, Ahmed? And you, Jasmine? You both were so eager to sacrifice another to take your place. What does that make you?"

"My motives were selfish enough," admitted, Ahmed. "I thought to protect Jasmine."

A familiar static brushed against Jasmine's leg and she glanced down to see Sheba butting her head against her leg, demanding attention.

"Who would protect her from *you* if I were gone? And Omar was no innocent. I had yet to prove it, but I know he was providing her uncle with young, underage girls. We've had him under surveillance at the hotel some time for other reasons, too."

"Not now, Sheba," Jasmine said softly, then supporting Ahmed's claims she added, "I knew he was a twisted bastard all along."

"Very tasty," confirmed the jinni. "Does it make you feel better about his demise?"

"No!" They both echoed.

"But don't you see, you would do the world a favor as well as yourselves. You will wed. A little white chapel perhaps? Together you shall sate my hunger. You will find vile and depraved souls for my feasting. Vegas is the perfect banquet hall for one such as me."

"What? We aren't even engaged." Jasmine said. "Ouch." She brushed Sheba away with her foot, annoyed that her beloved familiar had actually sunk her teeth into her ankle.

"You will be. Soon. Ahmed has loved you for a long time. Surely you know this. Tell her, Ahmed."

"This is not the time or place for such talk, and it's none of your business," Ahmed said, frowning. "What happened? Did Sheba bite you?" He reached toward the Siamese who instantly hissed and arched her back, striking out at him with her claw.

"Sheba! What has gotten into you?" Jasmine reached down and picked the cat up, snugging her against herself and the cat seemed to settle down.

"You are evading my questions, jinni," Jasmine said, turning her attention back to their current problem with her usual focus.

"Your mother and father made a bargain that they didn't keep. They wanted a child and would do anything to have it. I kept my end of the bargain. You are that child, Jasmine. And now you *will* fulfil their end of the bargain."

"Their end of the bargain? What did they owe you?"

"You know."

He was right. She knew. She knew the jinni's true addiction was dark, evil souls to feast upon. In her mindless desire to escape her uncle's clutches she had thought any price worth paying. Ahmed's cautions and begging for her to change her mind had fallen on deaf ears. Instead, she had dragged him, knowing all along how much he loved her, into the jinni's evil clutches, despite her good intentions. Jasmine looked at the opal ring and tried to pull it from her finger, but just as she had known all along it was there to stay.

Ahmed had been right. Jinn lied. She looked into his eyes, tears of regret running down her face. He reached down, tenderly wiping at them with a tissue. Then handed it to her, before pulling her against his side and letting her duck her head against his chest to cry.

Sheba let out a growl and hiss, and she glanced up. Angled against him, she chanced to see what looked like gratitude pass from Ahmed to the jinni, before he rested his cheek upon the top of her head and snuggled her gently, protectively in his arms.

She closed her eyes, blinded by tears, seeing more clearly at last with her third eye. The jinni hadn't trapped himself within the ring. He had enchanted the ring to enslave her, like her mother before her. Had he used her father to trap her mother as he was using Ahmed now? Was that the real reason her father drank?

A shudder caused her shoulders to tremble. Ahmed rubbed her back. It sent chills up her spine. Sheba hissed. Her uncle was a practice run. She was to endure the constant company of men so depraved and lecherous they wanted to perform illegal and bestial acts upon herself or the helpless victims they thought she would provide for them, night after night, as she lured them into the hands of a soul-sucking jinni. Perhaps Ahmed really believed that despite his obvious love and obsessive devotion to her, he would be able to endure a lifetime of protecting her from men like that so that their baser desires were left unfulfilled until the jinni's were met. But did he believe she could respect a man who would wish this life for her?

She felt Sheba's gentle connection as the cat rubbed her head against her neck and wondered what further secrets her psychic familiar was trying to reveal to her. Was it true what they said about the spirits of the dead returning in the form of the sacred cats? The feline purred loudly. Fine hairs along her neck rose.

"Get busy!"

Jasmine jumped, startled by the booming command.

"Cast your spells and entice your beasts, young sorceress. And keep her safe, Ahmed. I hunger!"

Rubbing her cheek against Sheba's velvety fur, she whispered, "I'm listening, mama."

Mary-Margaret Callahan's Perfect Day

Joseph J. Christiano

1.

The Plan

Mary-Margaret finished making the bed and stepped back. The added flourish of the folded corners of the pillowcases looked wonderful and made her smile. She had not seen those folded corners in years, not since Ed had made it a point to tell her how stupid they looked and to quit wasting her time with nonsense gestures. "You have other shit to do, Mary-Margaret. Best not to fiddly-fuck with pillowcases," Ed had told her. And so Mary-Margaret had abandoned the gesture for the first time in her life. That was seventeen years ago. Now she surveyed her handiwork and it reminded her of the time before Ed and their three-story Colonial outside Allentown. Before Josh was born, before she was forced to quit her job at the used bookstore and take one at the pharmaceutical company. Before everything. When her life was perfect.

Mary-Margaret turned from the bed with its folded pillowcases and caught a glimpse of herself in her dresser mirror. There was something different about her. Her hair, of course, which she had seen to last night, but there was something else. Not her pajamas or robe, all of which were old and threadbare. No, this was something subtle. She approached the mirror, studying her image intently. After another moment of staring, it dawned on her. She was smiling. The realization that such an expression should appear alien to her, so alien that it drew her attention, should have caused the smile to vanish and perhaps some tears to flow. Instead, Mary-Margaret leaned in closer to the mirror and studied the upturned corners of her mouth and watched the smile widen. She became aware that she had probably been smiling since the night before. As was usual for her, she had had no reason to smile.

Josh had thrown a fit when she told him they were out of mac and cheese. It was an honest mistake most likely caused by her son eating the last box and not telling her. She offered to make pasta, then pork chops, she even said she would go to the store and buy another box of mac and cheese. After another round of Josh telling her she was useless and the worst mother *ever*, Mary-Margaret had driven to the store and bought three small boxes of mac and cheese. Her son sat in front of the TV and ate in silence, shushing her when she tried to make conversation. There had been no thank you, no response of any kind. When he finished his supper he got up and tossed the plate into the sink and went up to his room. She did not see him the rest of the night.

Ed, at least, looked up from his paper a few times when the two of them sat at the table for their meal. Not that he said much, either, but any meal that ended with nothing being thrown her way was a good one. She curled up on the sofa with the latest Jenn Nixon hardcover while Ed drank beer and watched the Pirates blow out the Dbacks on TV. "Go, McCutchen!" he shouted after a long home run. Mary-Margaret was happy to see her husband happy. If nothing else his happiness would probably mean an uneventful night.

She knew she was wrong when she saw him enter the bedroom. He paused in the doorway and belched and wiped his chin. She peeked at him over the top of her novel and hoped he was too drunk to really want anything. God knew he was incapable of performing in his usual drunken state. And the fault was always hers. The last time he was unable to perform the result was a smack to her head. It did not hurt; he was too drunk to hit her squarely or put much behind the swing. After that he dozed off and snored.

He had the same look in his eyes last night. "Heya, babe," he mumbled. He staggered into the room and collapsed onto the bed. His hands groped blindly around her body.

Mary-Margaret put her book on the nightstand and lay back and waited for the inevitable explosion of rage when he realized nothing was happening south of the border. When he mounted her she braced herself. He surprised her by being hard already. She was further surprised when he entered her. It hurt, mostly because she was bone dry. He forced himself into her and his pace quickened when she gasped. His breath was warm on her face and neck and reeked of beer and weed. Mary-Margaret lay there and let Ed do his thing. It was over in a minute or two. He climbed off her and rolled onto his side and said nothing. Mary-Margaret felt his hot, wet discharge pool beneath her. She got out of bed and went into the bathroom and cleaned herself.

There had been no smile on her face, then. No smile, in fact, for many years. Not like the one she sported now. The one that most likely crept onto her features sometime after Ed passed out and she lay in bed and stared at the ceiling. The clock on her nightstand (always on hers, never his) read 3:18 when she started a mental checklist of what would constitute her Perfect Day. Within an hour she had most of the following day planned. And it started with the folded corners of the pillowcases.

Mary-Margaret exited the bedroom and went downstairs. The kitchen was empty. Ed was at work and Josh was most likely already playing his Xbox in his room, assuming he was even awake yet. That would be just fine. She preferred to be alone at this point in her Perfect Day.

She fixed his cereal. It was Lucky Charms, his favorite. When she got home from the store and showed him the box he had merely nodded and walked away. But on this Day, of all days, he would appreciate her purchase. And so would she. Mary-Margaret placed the bowl on the table in Josh's spot. She folded a paper napkin and put it next to the bowl and placed a spoon atop the napkin. Next she took his favorite drinking glass, the one with a black woman with dreadlocks and holding a samurai sword on one side and the logo for *The Walking Dead* on the other. She placed this glass top-down on the other side of the cereal bowl. Josh could have himself a nice bowl of Lucky Charms and a glass of milk when he came downstairs.

Then she took a shower. After that she got dressed for work. She allowed herself extra time because today she would wear makeup. Not a lot, mind you, but since Ed frowned on her wearing any makeup when she was outside his company, even this small amount would be noticeable to the people at the office. She fixed her hair in a very un-Mary-Margaret-like style, the same style she used to sport when she first met Ed. She had always liked her hair that way and by God she was going to wear it that way today.

Josh was still in his room when she pulled her Nissan out of the garage. She paused at the end of the driveway and looked at her house. Her eyes went to Josh's window and she could imagine him getting out of bed now that she was gone. Mary-Margaret knew he usually waited for her to leave before he came out and started his day. He would find the breakfast she left for him and he would eat and text and then it would be time to fire up the Xbox and get busy. "Whatever makes you happy, honey," she whispered. Then she was down the road and on her way to the office.

2.

Layton

The first parking spot next to those reserved for the president and vice-president was open, as it usually was this time of morning. Mary-Margaret never took that spot; it was the unofficial property of Amanda Layton, the office manager. Mary-Margaret put her Nisan perfectly between the two white lines. There would be hell to pay for that. "Good," Mary-Margaret whispered. "Good, good, good."

She waved a hello to Andrew, the elderly security guard, as she approached the front door. He smiled and held the door open for her.

"G'mornin, Mary-Margaret," he said with a wave back. "You did something different with your hair. Haircut?"

Mary-Margaret smiled. "I'm trying something different, Andrew. And thank you for noticing."

"Looks good on you. And what kind of day are you gonna have?" He asked the same question of her every morning, as he asked everyone.

She usually lied with "A great one" or something equally meaningless. Today was different. She paused and smiled again. "It's gonna be a *Perfect* Day, Andrew. Just *Perfect*."

He tilted his head slightly, a dog who has just heard an unfamiliar sound. He recovered quickly and his smile widened. "Glad to hear it, Mrs. Callahan, glad to hear it."

"Thanks, Andrew." She strode through the door and walked purposefully to the elevator. She rode up to three on her own. The old box creaked as it always did, as it always would. Mary-Margaret had never liked the elevator; she assumed if it was ever going to break down and plummet into the basement it would be with her inside. The thought did not even occur to her this time. If there was a God He would surely not allow such a thing to happen to her, not this Day of all days.

She got off on three and walked past reception into the main office area. She had the room to herself, and a quick glance at the clock told her she would for the next ten minutes. The girls would start to file in by then, with Ms. Layton being the last. Rank had its privileges, and screwing the boss in his office on a daily basis had even more. Mary-Margaret sat at her desk and turned on her desktop and started looking through her emails.

The time on her computer read 8:18 when Ms. Layton entered. The other girls nodded "Good morning" or "Hi, Ms. Layton." Mary-Margaret remained silent. There was no need to offer a greeting. Layton would surely want to speak with her about her choice of parking spot this morning.

Layton slowed as she neared Mary-Margaret's desk. She nearly came to a complete stop before she continued on to her own desk. Mary-Margaret chanced a glance over her shoulder and watched Layton go about her morning routine. The woman's body language spoke anger but she did not look in Mary-Margaret's direction. Had she just dodged a bullet? No, not possible. Women like Amanda Layton had an endless supply of ammunition with which to target office drones like Mary-Margaret. It dawned on her the woman was simply biding her time. They both knew Mary-Margaret's transgression and they both knew there would be a reckoning. The bitch was simply allowing Mary-Margaret to stew a little longer before she moved in for the kill. Let her take her time. Before the end of the day, probably before lunch, Layton would have more to be indignant about than her occupied parking space.

Mary-Margaret continued with her morning routine uninterrupted. At 8:58 Mr., Moore exited the elevator. The tall, young executive waved hello to the girls as he made his way to his office. Mary-Margaret greeted him with a friendly "Good morning, Mr. Moore" and a smile. He responded with a smile of his own. She tried to hold his eyes but he continued past too quickly.

She chanced another glance over her shoulder and saw Layton receive Moore's customary morning greeting of a nod and a smile. Layton smiled back and subtly licked her lips. It was a ridiculous charade. Mary-Margaret did not know how many others in the office knew the two were screwing their brains out behind the closed door to Moore's office but she suspected she was not alone. Moore and Layton were careful, but they were not *that* careful. Not that it would matter after today. By the time the office girls punched their timecards this afternoon there would be other topics of conversation.

Mary-Margaret waited until Mr. Moore closed the blinds to his office at 10:30. Then she pushed her chair back from her desk and stood. She eyed the closed blinds and imagined the man on the other side of them mentally and perhaps physically preparing himself for Layton's knock on the door. Mary-Margaret did a quick check of her hair and makeup in her compact. This was it. She steadied herself with a deep breath, put a smile on her lips, and walked to Moore's door. She did not look at Layton seated behind her desk but Mary-Margaret could not resist a peek at the woman's computer monitor. She saw the Amazon screen a moment before Layton minimized it, bringing up an Excel spreadsheet in its place. Mary-Margaret somehow kept her smile from widening.

She knocked on Moore's door. He said, "Yes?" from the other side. Mary-Margaret opened the door and stepped through. She closed it behind her, thumbing the lock quietly.

Moore was seated behind his rather large desk. Mary-Margaret's eyes scanned the room, lingering on the leather sofa on the wall to her right. How many hours, all told, did Layton spend on that sofa, legs spread and gasping for air as her lover pounded away at her? And there may yet be many more, but not today. Today would be different.

Moore looked up, managed to hide his surprise that it was not Layton standing at his door. Only his slightly-raised eyebrows betrayed him. He recovered quickly. "Mary-Margaret. What can I do for you?" He paused. "You do something with your hair?"

"I have a small problem, Mr. Moore," she began. She stepped away from the door slowly, tentatively. She faltered almost immediately. The part of her that was not at all down with The Perfect Day screamed at her to turn and run. If she could get to her car and traffic was with her she might even make it home before Josh got out of bed and went downstairs for his breakfast. This other part of her even suggested a few excuses she could feed Mr. Moore to explain her mad dash from his office.

No.

The force and finality of that one word echoed inside her head. She almost winced at the unexpected strength of the thought. *No no no.* This voice, from wherever it originated, was correct. She was not going to turn back now, not when her Perfect Day was about to truly start. She straitened her blouse and walked slowly and purposefully across the floor until she stood in front of Moore's desk.

Moore leaned back in his chair, regarded her. "What is it, Mary-Margaret? You look a little, I don't know, off, I guess."

"I feel a little off." She sauntered around the side of his desk and allowed her fingers to trace a path across its surface. She stopped at the corner and half-sat on the edge. She smiled in a way she had not since the earliest days of her marriage.

Moore was unable to hide his surprise. He sat as far back as his chair would allow. His hands went up in a double wave. "Mary-Margaret, what are you doing?" For the first time in her lengthy employment with Tavares Pharmaceuticals, the man did not sound like management. He seemed genuinely unsure of how to proceed.

Mary-Margaret's smile widened. "What I should have done a long time ago. What I've wanted to do for years." That was not entirely true but the lie would not bother her like it would have on any other day. She walked slowly around his chair, her fingers gliding along the leather. Her hand alighted gently on Moore's arm. The man froze and stuttered. "I know you want it, Mr. Moore. Charles. I want it, too."

Moore stuttered again. For the first time since he gave her the job, his air of Samuel L. Jackson cool slipped. He craned his neck to see Mary-Margaret standing behind him, looking down on him and smiling. "Mary-Margaret, you're married. What about Ed?"

Mary-Margaret nearly barked laughter. She managed to turn it into a soft giggle. "What about Talisha?" Moore swallowed nervously. Mary-Margaret liked Talisha Moore and it bothered her to know what the woman's husband was doing with Amanda Layton. But this was not about Talisha. This was about Layton, one-hundred-percent.

"People will talk." He did not sound convinced or even bothered by this notion.

Mary-Margaret completed her orbit around the high-backed leather chair and stopped in front of him. Slowly and gently, she lowered herself onto his lap. She draped one arm around his shoulders and placed her other hand on his chest. "Let them."

She leaned in and kissed him. Despite his pretense of surprise he kissed her back. He tasted like coffee, which was a far cry better than the beer-and-weed she usually tasted on Ed on the rare occasions he paid attention to her. She could smell his cologne, his aftershave. His tongue found its way into her mouth and she welcomed it. He pulled her closer, all pretense gone now, and she gave herself to him.

Mary-Margaret threw Moore's tie over his shoulder and worked the buttons on his shirt. When she reached the bottom she pulled the shirt up and tossed it to the side. Her hand found his belt and she had it loose with little effort. He kissed her more forcefully now, perhaps realizing she intended to see this through to its natural conclusion.

She broke away from his lips and kissed her way down his chest. He unbuttoned his slacks himself and dropped them to his knees. His boxers were black and made of silk. She remembered Layton at one of the company's Christmas parties talking of how she loved the feel of silk. That Moore wore these boxers for someone else today did nothing to dampen Mary-Margaret's mood; if anything it increased her excitement. She slid off the chair and knelt in front of Moore. She looked at him and smiled before she took him into her mouth.

He was already hard and he gasped when her lips closed around him. After only a few moments his breathing was quick and shallow. Mary-Margaret slowed and then stopped. "Not yet. You'd better wait."

He nodded quickly, his eyes lidded.

Mary-Margaret stood and took his hand. He looked both surprised and disappointed. "Come over here," she said softly. He stood and she led him to the black leather sofa. He kicked off his silk boxers and they sailed through the air and landed on the coatrack next to the office door.

Mary-Margaret pulled her blouse over her head and quickly unhooked her bra. She had wanted to take more time with this but it seemed Mr. Moore would not last as long as she hoped. She unzipped her skirt and let it slide down her legs; it pooled on the floor at her feet. Moore looked dumbly at it, then at her. Mary-Margaret smiled at him and crooked her finger.

Moore was on her instantly. He turned her around and gave her a gentle shove onto the sofa. Mary-Margaret got on all fours and awaited him. Moore did not disappoint in this, at least. He was behind her and a moment later she felt him enter her. Mary-Margaret gasped. He was a little bigger than she expected and he thrusted more forcefully than Ed ever managed. He felt good inside her. Not great, not even close to great, but good. And for this part of her Perfect Day, good was good enough.

Mary-Margaret moaned softly. It was only a half-ruse. She wanted Moore to make a bit more noise, to breathe heavier and perhaps make the sofa springs creak their protest, anything that might make Layton, who was surely on the other side of the door, realize what was happening; she also wanted to encourage the man to use more force. She was not close to orgasm, not yet, but she was on her way.

The sofa springs did creak, but softly, probably not enough to make it to Layton's ears. Mary-Margaret dug in a little more, willing the damn things to make noise. Moore, for his part, was putting everything he had into this. His breathing had become gasping, his fingers dug into her hips. Surely he would leave bruises but she was okay with that. She would consider them mementoes of her Perfect Day.

Moore's next thrust was particularly vicious and deep. Mary-Margaret gasped and moaned more loudly than she intended. He must have found her reaction quite satisfactory; he began to pound his way deeper inside her. Mary-Margaret found herself leaning back, encouraging him. Her orgasm began to build and she reached back and grabbed his ass, forcing him to move faster. It took only a moment more.

Mary-Margaret felt herself explode. Every muscle in her body contracted at once. She tried to scream but she seemed unable to produce any sound at all. She found herself in a sea of delusional ecstasy, alone in all the world for that single moment. Her body shuddered and her arms nearly buckled. She caught herself in time to stop from face-planting into the leather.

"Jesus Christ," Moore gasped.

Mary-Margaret barely heard him. The strength of her orgasm had drained her. She lowered herself gently and placed her head on the sofa's armrest.

Moore exited her. Mary-Margaret wanted to protest but she had trouble forming words. She allowed him to turn her over, onto her back. Her lungs worked double time, taking in great gulps of air.

"God *damn*, Mary-Margaret, you're full of surprises today."

"Shut up and fuck me," she managed. The phrase surprised her as much as Moore. She had never said that before, not even to Ed back when she thought their marriage meant something. Her boss was correct; she was indeed full of surprises this day.

Moore mounted her and a moment later he was inside her again. Mary-Margaret lay there and waited for him to finish. She was too drained to give him much encouragement beyond a few weak moans. A few moments later his thrusting and his breathing quickened. He leaned down and kissed her. Mary-Margaret turned her head and gave him her cheek. His breathing stopped suddenly. He moaned loudly, certainly loud enough for anyone on the other side of the door to hear him.

Mary-Margaret smiled.

At last Moore was spent. He slid off the edge of the sofa and sat on his office floor. His chest heaved and sweat coated his forehead and chest. Mary-Margaret lay on the sofa, out of breath and covered with sweat and her boss's juices. She lay there motionless for several moments, collecting herself.

For the first time in her life she had just had sex with a man who was not Ed. The thought of doing it had never even occurred to her before last night. She did not feel shame nor regret, two emotions with which the old Mary-Margaret would certainly be awash, lying naked on her boss's sofa, her new hairdo plastered to her skull with sweat. But this Mary-Margaret, the new and improved Mary-Margaret, felt oddly calm and fulfilled. It wasn't the orgasm, as powerful as it was; this was something different. No, not just different. This was *alien*. The realization both startled and energized her.

Moore recovered first. He stumbled to his private bathroom and emerged a moment later, toweling his chest and abdomen and giving his still-hard rod a good once-over. He tossed a second towel to her. "That was fucking amazing."

She nodded absently and cleaned herself.

"I don't know where that came from but I'd be happy to do that again," Moore said to her as he finished buttoning his shirt. He appeared professional again, aside from the last beads of sweat that still clung to his shaved head. He picked up his tie and walked to Mary-Margaret and kissed her on her forehead. "Thank you."

Mary-Margaret shrank from the gesture and reached for her panties and skirt. She pulled them on in silence and gave herself a quick inspection in the mirror above the wet bar. She had left one elongated drop of evidence on her upper chest, and she was careful not to smear it when she put on her bra and blouse. Her hair was a bit of a mess but she fixed it easily enough. Her makeup was still perfect.

Moore was back behind his desk. He looked up from his computer monitor and motioned her over with a smile. She walked to him slowly, mostly to recover her shoes on the side of his desk. "I meant it, we really need to do that again," he told her. He placed his arm around her waist and pulled her closer. "What do you think?"

Mary-Margaret sat on his lap and put on her shoes. "We'll see." It was another lie, her second in the past fifteen minutes. She did not care. She stood and walked to his door. She did not pause on her way through and she closed it behind her.

Layton was at her desk but she was not working. She glared at Mary-Margaret with surprise and hatred. Mary-Margaret knew the bitch had been listening at the door for most of the time she had been inside Moore's office.

Mary-Margaret smiled. This was also part of her Perfect Day.

She walked past Layton's desk. As she did she retrieved the last of Moore's ejaculate with her finger and she smeared in on Layton's computer monitor. "Good morning, Ms. Layton." Mary-Margaret did not wait for a reaction beyond Layton's initial shocked gasp. She continued on her way to the ladies room.

Mary-Margaret entered and walked to the closest sink. She wet a few paper towels under the tap and dabbed her forehead and neck. She paid closer attention to the small streak of Moore's ejaculate left behind by her finger before she spread the rest of it on Layton's monitor. She was in the process of cleaning up the last of it when the door opened. Mary-Margaret did not look up. There was no need. She knew who was there.

"You fucking *bitch*."

Mary-Margaret continued to clean up the last of the mess. "I'd watch that if I were you, Mandy."

"Mand—" Layton gasped.

Mary-Margaret tossed the wadded paper towels into the trash and washed her hands over the sink.

Layton recovered from her surprise a little more slowly than Mary-Margaret anticipated. She was clearly in shock at this morning's events. She sputtered, her hands clenching and unclenching. Her shoulders shook. "Who do you think you're talking to?"

Mary-Margaret took a few more paper towels and dried her hands.

"I asked you a question." Layton seemed to gather herself a bit more. She advanced two steps into the ladies room. "Who do you think you're talking to? I'm your boss. I could fire you any time I want. And I know what you just did in Mr. Moore's office."

"Well, I hope so," Mary-Margaret replied. "I tried to be as obvious as I could." She faced Layton and gave the woman a wry smile. "So obvious even you could figure it out."

Layton sputtered again. "How about I fire your ass, you fucking slut? How about that?"

Mary-Margaret shrugged. "Knock yourself out. But I think Mr. Moore might have something to say about it." She remained in place, half-leaning against the vanity with her arms folded across her chest. Her body language was casual, cool; they might have been sharing recipes or making plans for a girls night out. "He said he wanted to do it again. I think he was rather pleased with the results of our meeting."

Layton's face transitioned to purple. The veins in her forehead bulged, her arms quivered. She tried to speak but it seemed her rage robbed her of the ability to produce sounds.

Mary-Margaret stood and walked to Layton. She did not stop until their noses were a few inches apart. "I just fucked your man." Her voice was level, calm. "I fucked him on that black leather sofa of his. And before that, I blew him at his desk. And, lest we forget, I also took your parking spot." Then her voice dropped an octave. She leaned in even closer to Layton. "What the fuck are you gonna do about it?" She paused for a breath. "Bitch."

Layton's eyes bugged. Mary-Margaret would not have been surprised if they popped out of the woman's head. Her lips worked but she was still incapable of producing sound, much less coherent words.

Mary-Margaret waited. She remained in place, her nose separated from Layton's by no more than a fee centimeters. The younger woman shook with rage but she made no move against Mary-Margaret. Perhaps she was also incapable of movement.

Satisfied, Mary-Margaret backed up a step. Layton remained motionless. Mary-Margaret turned her attention to the mirror above the sink and began to fix her hair. "You've been fucking him for how long now? Two years, at least. And that's fine. You can go on fucking him every day and twice on Sunday for all I care. But if you ever threaten me again, or try to lord it over me and the other girls…" She stepped away from the mirror and turned back to Layton. "They'll never find your fucking body. Do I make myself clear, Ms. Layton?"

Some of the rage seemed to drain from the younger woman. She stood still as a statue, eyes still locked on Mary-Margaret. But the anger, the utter hatred, had been replaced by something else.

Fear? Oh yes, definitely that. Perhaps even a little more than fear. Her lips trembled but it was no longer with rage. It occurred to Mary-Margaret that this was an Amanda Layton she had never before seen. For the first time since Layton started her tenure in the office she seemed utterly lost, maybe even submissive.

Mary-Margaret raised her hand and watched with satisfaction as Layton shrunk away from it. She hesitated, smiled, and tapped Layton gently on her cheek. "That's my girl." Mary-Margaret exited the ladies room without looking over her shoulder.

As she walked past Layton's desk her eyes were drawn to the computer monitor. It was clean. Mary-Margaret smiled again and returned to her desk. It was a full five minutes before Layton emerged from the ladies room. She walked slowly to her desk, eyes down, and sat silently. She glanced quickly at Mary-Margaret but averted her gaze when her look was returned.

Mary-Margaret went about her morning routine, filing reports and sending emails. She downed two cups of coffee and took her first break in the employee lounge. She skimmed through the day's paper and sipped her coffee. She half-expected Layton to show up, back to her usual self and ready for round two. It never happened. Nancy, one of the office girls, came in and took her break. They discussed the weather before the girl asked if everything was okay. The office girls watched Layton storm into the ladies room and they all expected to hear shouting and perhaps objects being thrown about. Mary-Margaret smiled and told her no, they had had a pleasant conversation and all was well. Nancy looked skeptical but she did not press the issue.

Mary-Margaret returned to her desk and worked steadily until noon. Then she stood and walked to Layton's desk. The woman froze for a moment before she slowly looked up. "Yes?"

"I'm taking the rest of the day off, Ms. Layton." Mary-Margaret's voice was steady, even pleasant. "I have a big day and night ahead of me."

"Of course," Layton replied too quickly. "Of course you can have the rest of the day. We'll see you tomorrow."

Mary-Margaret nodded. She returned to her desk and gathered up her things. On the way out she looked into Mr. Moore's office. He was behind his desk, talking on his phone. He smiled and waved at Mary-Margaret. She did not return the gesture.

Her eyes lingered on the black leather sofa. There was nothing to suggest anything had happened a few hours earlier. She closed her eyes and tried to bring back the sensation of being on all fours with her boss pounding her from behind. She found she could not. Her memory seemed as cleansed of the incident as was the sofa. But Moore would remember. And so would Layton. And that was enough.

Andrew was still at his post when she exited the building. He waved to her and said, "Have an errand to run, Mrs. Callahan?"

Mary-Margaret shook her head. "No, Andrew. Calling it a day."

"Everything's okay, I hope."

Mary-Margaret smiled. "Never better, Andrew. Never better."

She walked to her car, noting with some satisfaction that Layton's new Camaro was parked at the far end of the row, as far from the front doors as the lot would allow. Mary-Margaret resisted the urge to key the thing and got into her Nissan. A moment later she was on her way home.

3.

Josh

Mary-Margaret pulled into her driveway and shut off the Nissan. She got out and looked at her son's bedroom window. The blinds were still drawn. He could still be asleep, but odds were he was on his Xbox playing one of the various war games he so enjoyed. It was possible he had been up there all morning, even eschewing breakfast in the name of digital violence and death. She paused then, unsure of what she should do if Josh had indeed not left his room yet. In the end she decided it did not matter. Nothing was going to spoil her Perfect Day. Not even her son.

With her Nissan parked in the garage Mary-Margaret entered her home through the kitchen. Josh's breakfast was indeed still awaiting his arrival. She walked into the living room and craned her neck toward the ceiling and listened intently. Faintly, above the steady *click-click* of the mantle clock above the fireplace, she could hear the sound of explosions and gunfire from the room above.

Interrupting his game to ask about breakfast would only anger him. Josh had certain rules when it came to his game time (and his TV time, his studying time, his texting time) and Rule Number One was no interruptions. Mary-Margaret looked at the clock. She had plenty of time before Ed came home, four hours, at least, but she began to doubt if Josh would ever come down. And if he did, would he even want his cereal and milk? If he decided he was not in the mood for breakfast food it could ruin her Perfect Day. Mary-Margaret decided to chance it.

She walked up the stairs and paused at her son's door. She could hear the explosions much more clearly, could even hear her son swearing at the screen. She raised her hand to knock on the door, hesitated. One deep breath later, Mary-Margaret knocked on Josh's door and opened it a crack.

He sat on the edge of his bed, leaning his body left and then right, clicking away at the controller. His TV showed enemy soldiers being blown to pieces in the shattered remains of a city. Each explosion resulted in severed limbs shooting across the screen. Josh celebrated each such death with a half-whispered "Yes!" or "Fuck yeah!" Mary-Margaret would have frowned on such language if she did not hear it on a daily basis from both him and her husband.

She opened the door the rest of the way and stood at the threshold. She cleared her throat. Josh continued his path of digital destruction. Mary-Margaret cleared her throat again, much more loudly.

Josh half-turned, did a double-take when he saw his mother standing in the doorway, arms folded across her chest. "Mom? What are you doing home?" He immediately returned his attention to his game.

"I took the rest of the day off, honey. I wanted to spend some time with you. I don't think we do enough of that anymore."

Josh's only reply was a quick shake of his head. Even with his back to her she knew he was rolling his eyes and silently cursing her intrusion. In fact, his lack of a verbal scolding for interrupting his game time threw Mary-Margaret for a moment. She stuttered, licked her lips.

"Come on downstairs. I fixed breakfast for you. You should eat something."

"Busy," he said. His fingers flew across his controller. More soldiers died horrible deaths on the TV. He sounded impatient but not quite angry. It occurred to her Josh was probably high.

She could smell nothing out of the ordinary in his room but he was too smart for that, anyway. Even with the house to himself he would not be stupid enough to smoke anything, just on the off-chance someone came home early. He would have gone out back where the yard was bordered by large shrubs and trees. He would be invisible to the neighbors back there, invisible to anyone walking or driving by. He probably learned that from his father. Ed was careful when it came to his weed but Josh could (and probably had) observed his father out back from the bathroom window. Mary-Margaret frowned.

"Come on, honey, get something to eat. You can't go all day without eating something. It's not healthy."

"Mom, what the fuck." He did not turn away from the game. "I'm busy, okay? I'll get something later."

Mary-Margaret was used to the way Josh spoke to her. It had been going on since he was about twelve-years-old. She had tried, with no help from Ed, to break him of that habit. Eventually she gave up. But on this day, this Perfect Day, she bristled in a way she had not for the last three years. Her first instinct was to march across the room and rip the controller from his hands and smack the shit out of him. She smiled at the image that produced in her mind. He would be stunned, at least initially. From there his reaction could go either way. Beating the hell out of her son certainly appealed to her, this day of all days, but that was not part of her plan. Instead, she said, simply, "I'll wait for you downstairs. You can finish what you're doing but I'll expect you at the kitchen table right after that."

Josh did not reply. Mary-Margaret closed his door and went down to the kitchen.

She sat at the table in her usual chair, her hands folded in her lap. Her eyes wandered from the cereal bowl to the window above the sink. Every so often she would glance at the Mickey Mouse clock on the wall next to the table. The only sound was the *click-click* of Mickey's tail making the rounds on the clock face and the background hum of the refrigerator. Mary-Margaret sat in silence, unmoving, waiting for her son.

Mickey told her it was 1:10 PM when she heard Josh's door open. Her eyes tracked his progress into the bathroom. A few moments later she heard the toilet flush. She held her breath. If he returned to his room and that fucking game her Perfect Day would most likely be at an end. And while showing up Layton had been fun, invigorating, even, it was not enough to make her day Perfect. For that she needed Josh.

Her heart skipped a beat when she heard his footsteps on the stairs. A smile worked its way onto her lips. She erased it with some effort.

Josh entered the kitchen and stopped in his tracks when he saw her. His face fell. "Jesus Christ. I thought you were asleep in your room or something. What are you doing sitting in here all alone?"

His tone was accusatory and she knew why instantly. His eyes had been focused on the back door before he saw her. His right hand curled into a tight fist but she could see the bottom of the lighter poking out.

"I was waiting for you, honey." Her smile returned. She indicated the cereal bowl with her hand. "You really need to eat something. Josh." *You can't survive on weed alone,* she thought but did not say. "It's not healthy to starve yourself."

Josh slipped his hand into his pocket. He probably thought she had seen nothing, that he was slick enough or she was stupid enough not to notice. Mary-Margaret simply chose to ignore the gesture. She was more interested in his next move.

He looked angry, as he usually did around her. But he also looked a bit relieved, as if he had just dodged a bullet. He approached the table and pulled out his chair with more force than was necessary. "Whatever." He plopped himself down and regarded the cereal bowl. "Am I supposed to eat this shit without milk?"

Mary-Margaret smiled pleasantly and got up from the table. She returned with the milk and poured it for him. She filled his *The Walking Dead* glass nearly to the top before she returned the milk to the fridge. Then she was back in her chair.

Josh shoveled a spoonful of Lucky Charms into his mouth and chewed with his mouth half-open. Most of the cereal was gone before he paused and looked up. Mary-Margaret sat in her chair with her smile firmly in place. He frowned and returned his attention to the bowl. His relief at having not been caught was gone now, replaced by his usual open contempt for all things Mary-Margaret Callahan.

"How is it, honey?"

Josh grunted. He finished off the cereal and then the milk. He belched quite loudly, enough to startle her had she not been prepared for it. Then he pushed himself back from the table and stood. He glanced at the clock before he left the kitchen and headed back upstairs.

Mary-Margaret stood and cleared the table. Her smile widened as she washed the bowl and glass.

She walked into the living room and plopped down on the sofa. It was not leather, nor was it black, but she flashed back to the sofa in Mr. Moore's office and what had occurred there this morning. She became aware of something damp between her legs. Not quite subconsciously, Mary-Margaret began to touch herself.

This, too, was alien to her. She had never masturbated in her life. She had the urge from time to time but she had always managed to squash it. It was not something a married mother-of-one should do. Her sexual appetite had to be satisfied by her husband. In the early days that had not been a problem, but by the third year of their marriage, Ed had provided her with fewer and fewer occasions for release. As her fingers went to work she wondered why in the world she had never done this before. Well, *that* was certainly going to change from now on. The new and improved Mary-Margaret would get what she needed, even if she had to do the deed herself.

She sat in her living room and masturbated gently and listened to the squirrels squawking in the big maple in the front yard. Her body shuddered when she brought herself to orgasm. She sat on the sofa and tried to catch her breath. After a moment she surveyed the sofa. There was a wet spot on the fabric but not a large one. Fabric cleaner and a dishrag would take care of that. The thought occurred to her that for the first time in her life she had had two orgasms in one day. And it was not even 2 PM yet. Mary-Margaret sat back down and turned on the Food Network and waited.

It was perhaps fifteen minutes later when she heard something upstairs. She glanced in that direction but remained still otherwise. She heard heavy footsteps and then Josh's door banged open. "Mom!" Silence for a moment, then, louder than the first, "*MOM*!"

Mary-Margaret returned her attention to the television.

More heavy footsteps. They stutter-stepped across the upstairs hallway. Mary-Margaret mentally tracked her son's progress. He would be near the bathroom now. She heard a loud thud, his legs buckling and landing him on his knees on the bathroom linoleum.

"MOM!" She heard him vomit and hoped he made it to the toilet. Mary-Margaret grabbed up the remote and lowered the TV's volume. She could live without seeing it but she could not deprive herself of the sounds.

More stumbling upstairs. Josh made it back into the hallway. He screamed for her again. Another loud thud followed by whimpering. A strange squeaking. It took her a moment to realize he was pulling himself along the hardwood toward the stairs.

Mary-Margaret's eyes went from the TV to the staircase. On the wall she could make out her son's shadow. It was low to the ground and moving slowly. Mary-Margaret looked back to the TV.

"MOM!"

One of Josh's hands made an appearance on the stairs, followed by its twin a moment later. When his arms came into view Mary-Margaret could see they were shaking with the effort. Her eyes travelled back to the TV.

"I'm here, honey." Her voice was pleasant, even warm.

"Mom, help! I'm sick!"

Mary-Margaret watched one of the celebrity chefs preparing a chicken/linguini dish that looked wonderful.

Josh lost traction and slid down the stairs. He managed to catch himself before the bottom but not before his head collided with one of the steps. Instinctively his hands went to his head. He tumbled down the last few steps and landed in a heap at the base. His body shook as if he were outside in mid-January. "Mom." His voice was a strangled whisper.

"I'm here, honey," Mary-Margaret told him.

Josh twisted his body around until he could see her. His eyes, thin slits wet with fear, blossomed into saucers when he saw her. His mouth worked but he seemed unable to produce anything beyond a muffled grunt. He reached for her with one outstretched arm; his other hand clutched his abdomen tightly. "M…M…"

Mary-Margaret shifted her position on the sofa. She locked eyes with Josh and held his gaze.

Josh spasmed and shit himself. His body convulsed violently. His limbs worked themselves into a position a professional contortionist would find enviable. He reached for his mother again. Tears streamed down his cheeks and pattered onto the hardwood.

Mary-Margaret continued to hold his gaze. She smiled her most pleasant mommy smile. Josh shuddered again. His fingers curled into a fist and he lay his head on the floor. Mary-Margaret closed her eyes and listened to his staccato breathing. It ceased with a long, slow exhale and sounded to her ears like air escaping from a punctured tire. For several moments the only sound within the living room was the commercial for Tide laundry detergent. When at last Mary-Margaret opened her eyes she turned her head slightly and regarded her son.

Josh lay where last she saw him. His eyes were large and fixed on her. His mouth was open wide and a string of spittle connected it to the floor. His hand still reached for her. He made no sounds now, no movements of any kind. He simply lay in his own shit and piss at the base of the stairs.

Mary-Margaret stood and looked at her little boy. Josh did not react to her at all. He remained frozen and silent.

Mary-Margaret knelt beside him. She brushed a lock of stray hair from his eyes and looked at him. For a moment, only a moment, he was newborn again. She held him in her arms while he cooed and looked at her with wide eyes. The moment passed quickly and Mary-Margaret was back in her living room with her dead son sprawled at her feet.

She went upstairs and changed into her sweatpants and a tee-shirt.

4.

The Cleanup

She rolled the body up in the Oriental rug Ed insisted on buying when they first moved into the house. Mary-Margaret had always hated this fucking rug although she could not have said why, other than it was ugly and a waste of money. At last, after twelve years, the goddamned thing was serving a purpose. Once Josh was snug inside Mary-Margaret dragged the heavy and bulky thing into the kitchen. She set it down long enough to open the backdoor and then she and her son were outside.

The shrubs and trees that lined the backyard stood sentinel. Ed had demonstrated the privacy they provided when he lured her into the backyard on a warm night in August of '06 and took her to the ground and fucked her. Even then, so many years away from the morning she would get the idea for her Perfect Day, she had never fooled herself into thinking her husband made love to her. That was for other couples, those with love and respect for one another. Ed Callahan was not that kind of man. But the lesson was learned. Mary-Margaret could go to work back here without much worry the neighbors would see anything.

She dragged her son's corpse into the middle of the yard and laid it down gently on the grass. A moment later she was inside the shed. She found the shovels Ed bought at Lowe's a few years ago and took them both. They had seen little action since their purchase, Ed not being known for his love of landscaping. A pair of thick work gloves lay on the shelf above the shovels. Mary-Margaret took those, too, and returned to the backyard.

She chose a spot near the edge of the woods that bordered the back of the property. There was little grass there but there was plenty of debris from the trees that could be useful. She took the bigger of the two shovels and went to work.

The top soil was easy enough to remove but she had penetrated only a few inches below it before she started hitting rocks. None of them were particularly large but there were many. Each time the shovel found another one the impact produced an unpleasant sound and sent tremors up her arms. She paused only twice, once to wipe her face and neck with her shirt and once for a quick trip to the bathroom. It took two hours to produce a space big enough in which to bury her son.

The grave was shallow, no more than four feet deep, tops. It was uneven, with its deepest point being in the middle and tapering up at both ends. She knew she should go deeper but exhaustion threatened to stop her if she tried. She was also filthy and her arms and back ached and promised much pain for tomorrow. And she had the clock to consider. Ed would be home in another two hours. She should have enough time to prepare for his return but not if she wanted a deeper grave for her son. She decided the grave was good enough as-is and went to retrieve her son's body.

She noted it took more effort to drag the rug across the yard than it had to take it from the house. Her muscles protested and Mary-Margaret grunted with the effort. At last she had it at the edge of the grave. She sank to her knees and shoved the rug with both hands. It rolled over the edge, unfolding as it went. Josh's head and one of his arms escaped before the body came to rest. He stared at the sky with wide eyes and mouth still agape.

"Sleep tight, honey," she whispered, as she had so often when he was younger.

She scooped up the shovel and tossed the first load of dirt onto her son's face. Some of it landed in his eyes, his mouth. Mary-Margaret did not stop until all the dirt was replaced. The ground rose a foot or so above the rest of the area. It was noticeable but she was not bothered. One good soaking rain would level most of it. She thought she might even buy some seeds and plant flowers over the grave. It would certainly add some color to the backyard.

Mary-Margaret tamped down the loose dirt atop the grave. After that she hosed off the shovels and returned them to their place in the shed. She was sore and sweaty and dirty. A hot shower sounded like heaven. She went back inside.

She paused in the living room. The spot where her son died was wet with piss and small droplets of half-dried blood. The smell was bad and too obvious to be missed by anyone. Her shower would have to wait.

Mary-Margaret scrubbed the area with bleach and hot water. She lit an incense stick she found in Josh's room and sprayed some air freshener. Then she opened the bay window and was greeted by a warm, pleasant breeze. She closed her eyes and let it flow around and through her. The sweat on her skin felt cool and some gooseflesh rose on her arms. Mary-Margaret breathed deeply and slowly.

Then she was back in Josh's room. It was a wreck, as it always was. She began with the clothes strewn in various places about the room. There was no way to know which were clean so she consigned them all to the hamper. She could afford to run them through the wash one more time before she gave them to Goodwill.

She found several plates and bowls, forks and spoons. They went atop the clothes in the hamper. She organized his video games and his flash drives. After that she cleaned the search history from his desktop, watching with some satisfaction as a few dozen porn sites disappeared from the list.

She found his stash of weed quite by accident. She had known Josh was smoking but any inquiry on her part would have been met with hostility and she had had enough of that in her life. Now she held the proof in her hand. Mary-Margaret had been drunk once,

New Year's Eve back in '97, but she had never been stoned. She looked at the small baggie with the buds inside, the small black glass pipe nestled among them.

"Why the hell not?" she asked the empty room. She still had a little more than an hour before Ed came home. And she knew just how and where to spend that time.

A few moments later she was running a bath. She added the lilac bubble bath to the water and breathed deeply. Her clothes went in a heap on the tiled floor. When she stepped into the tub and lowered herself into the warm, scented water, she lay back and closed her eyes. She remained that way for several moments before she washed the sweat and dirt from her body. She took her time, something she had been unable to do for years.

When she felt clean she lay back again. She picked up the baggie she found in her son's room and looked at it. Then she reached inside and withdrew the small pipe. The bowl was full, although the top layer of green was singed black. Mary-Margaret poked at it and turned over the bowl's contents until she saw only green. She brought the pipe to her mouth and readied Josh's lighter. She hesitated.

She had never partaken of an illegal substance in her life. Even when she and Ed were dating and he was smoking this shit daily, she had never caved to the pressure to join him. And now, here she was. "Fuck it," she whispered, and brought the lighter to life.

She coughed on the first hit, barely-inhaled smoke exploding from her lungs. Mary-Margaret coughed and grimaced. Christ, it tasted like shit. How did people do this on a regular basis? She started to put it away but instead brought the pipe back up and tried again. It scorched her throat even worse on the second hit. She coughed out the green smoke, dropping the glass pipe on the floor as she did. She coughed a few more times, felt the burning sensation in her chest. Nope, this kind of thing was not for her.

She looked over the side, saw the pipe lying in two pieces on the tiled floor. Well, that was okay. She had no plans to give it another go. She stepped out of the tub and reached for the towel. When she was dry she picked up the broken pipe and tossed it into the small trash pail to the side of the vanity. Then she brushed her teeth. The toothpaste did little to rid her of the disgusting taste of weed so she tried some mouthwash next. It helped, made the lingering aftertaste a little easier to tolerate.

She was getting dressed a few minutes later when she realized she felt strange. It took her several moments to conclude the little amount of smoke she inhaled, and the miniscule amount of time it spent in her lungs, had done its job, after all. She giggled when she realized she was high for the first time in her life. She felt good, relaxed, the most relaxed she had felt in years, perhaps even decades. Maybe weed was her thing, after all.

The glass pipe was broken, but she was sure she would be able to procure another. There was a headshop over on Albany Ave that would have a selection. She could probably find a dealer when Josh's stash ran out; there were a few people at the office known to indulge. Mary-Margaret lay on her bed with her arms spread like wings and closed her eyes and enjoyed the effects of the smoke.

She nearly drifted off. She started suddenly, looked at the clock next to the bed. Ed would be home in less than an hour. And she still had a few things to do before he arrived.

She sat up too quickly and her head swam. Mary-Margaret moaned and lay back down. Apparently there was a downside to weed aside from the disgusting taste. She closed her eyes and counted down from ten. She still felt woozy but she had things to do. Even this temporary setback was not going to ruin her Perfect Day.

She sat up slowly and swung her feet off the bed. Still woozy, still dizzy, but the clock was ticking. She stood, swayed a little. *Good God, how did Josh do this shit all the time?* Sure, it felt great so long as one did not move too much. But she had to move, and quickly.

Mary-Margaret went downstairs with one hand on the wall just in case. She entered the garage and ransacked Ed's toolbox. She reentered the house with her arms full, mentally checking off each item carried. She had a good idea which one should go where, based on her estimate of where Ed would be when the time presented itself. It took about thirty minutes to place the tools around the house and to ensure they would not be seen easily. When the garage door began to squeal its way up the track Mary-Margaret plopped down on the sofa and opened the nearest magazine.

5.

Family Life

They met on a double date. Her friend Ally was dating Ed's brother Bill. That relationship lasted about as long as Hitler's marriage, but she and Ed surprised everyone by continuing theirs. They dated for the better part of a year before he proposed. He drank a bit too much for her taste, and he was high a lot, but mostly he was a good man. And she was in love with him, after all.

Their first year of marriage was the best. Ed paid attention to her, spoke with her (instead of at her), they did a little travelling that summer, and sex was often and mostly satisfying. Even then she stopped short of calling it "making love" but she did enjoy it. It took all of four months before she was pregnant with Josh. Looking back, that was the first real crack in the armor of their marriage.

Ed wanted her to terminate the pregnancy. "We ain't ready to have kids," he would say, often and with greater and greater anger. "Once there's a rug rat running around here, that's the end of this lifestyle. No more going out, no more vacations, no more anything."

She had argued with him. From the perspective of sixteen years later, she could not believe she had ever had the nerve to stand up to him. She pointed to their friends who had children. They still went out, they had a social life. Money was tight for some of them but they managed. She really wanted to be a mother, had wanted it her whole life. So *please*, Ed, let's not fight about this.

He did not hit her, then, but he came close. The anger in his eyes, his shoulders shaking with rage, he brought up one of his hands and she backed away. He thought better of it, stormed up the stairs and slammed their bedroom door closed. And she stood in the living room, eyes wet and hands trembling.

The following day she went to Kmart and bought clothes two sizes too big for her. Her belly would be growing soon, and she did not want the constant reminder of their impending parenthood in Ed's face every day for the next seven months.

He spoke to her with less frequency the closer she got to giving birth to their son. As he drove her to the hospital on the day Josh was born, he did not speak to her at all. He held his son at the hospital, but Mary-Margaret knew it was a show for the candy stripers. Once they were home Ed spent little time with the baby.

He stayed out after work on most nights. He would come home stinking of alcohol and weed. Sometimes she caught the scent of a woman's perfume on him. Mary-Margaret did her best to be a good wife to him while giving most of her attention to their new child. The sex continued but it was sporadic and not particularly noteworthy, not for her, anyway.

The first time he hit her was two months and three days after Josh's birth. She burned the pork chops because the baby threw up and she had to attend to him. He used an open hand that time, slapping the shit out of her and knocking her down. Mary-Margaret gaped at him in total shock, holding one hand to her cheek and mouth and tasting blood, holding the other hand out in a protective gesture. Then he sat down at the table and ate in silence.

That incident seemed to open the floodgates. After that Ed never thought twice about dispensing a little physical punishment if he thought the transgression warranted such. Mary-Margaret learned to apply makeup in such a way to hide bruises. The few times he made her limp she explained it away as having banged her knee on the end table or the car door. No one, not even her mother, questioned her explanations.

By the time they celebrated Josh's seventh birthday she and Ed had settled into a familiar routine. The sex had stopped—for her, anyway; Ed seemed to do just fine with whomever he was meeting after work—any conversation was perfunctory and to the point. They entertained friends and family rarely. When they were forced to do so Ed was always pleasant, even patting her ass once in front of Bill and his family. And when they were alone once more he would either go upstairs to watch TV in the bedroom or go out to get laid.

The physical abuse continued. Sometimes he would wait until Josh was elsewhere, sometimes he would slap her in front of the boy. Josh would cry and scream. Once he even threw a few weak punches at his father's legs to stop him. Ed ignored the boy until he was finished with Mary-Margaret; then it was Josh's turn. Mostly he would get a smack, sometimes a punch, always on his head where the boy's hair would hide any bruises. Ed knew Mary-Margaret would keep quiet but the boy's teachers would be another matter. And it simply would not do to involve anyone outside the family in what Ed considered a private matter.

Josh started to drift away from her by the time he turned eleven-years-old. By thirteen he had no use for his mother beyond her motherly duties of feeding him and keeping his clothes washed and folded. The verbal abuse he hurled at her matched anything she received from Ed.

She complained to her husband only once. "If you're too much of a pussy to control your own son, you deserve what you get from him," was Ed's reply. "Fucking kid needs to get the shit kicked out of him. You need to discipline that boy, Mary-Margaret. It won't mean the same if I do it. He's already afraid of me. You don't hear him saying that shit to me, do you? No, only you, because he knows he can get away with it. He's an asshole because of you."

After a while she stopped questioning anything Josh did. Ed was no help, stepping in only when Josh's actions interfered with what he, Ed, wanted. Josh learned very quickly there was no standing up to his father. Ed was right about that, at least. But the boy would then take out his anger on Mary-Margaret as soon as his father was out of the house. Then he would go to his room and play video games or text his friends or get high, sometimes all three at the same time. Ed would be out with one of his mistresses. And Mary-Margaret would lie in her bed and cry.

She took her office job as a means of keeping her sanity. Ed was indifferent to her decision, stipulating only that her schedule had better not interfere with her responsibilities around the house. She kept the place clean and dinner was never late and so Ed never had much to say about her day job.

Her life improved, at least for a while. Having the job gave Mary-Margaret a sense of self-worth she had not felt since she and Ed were dating. Then Amanda Layton was hired and even her daytime refuge turned to shit. Mary-Margaret simply had nowhere to go.

Early last night Mary-Margaret sat on the edge of her bed with her wedding photo in her right hand and an old straight razor in her left. The photo came from the mantle downstairs; the razor she found in a box of Ed's old things in the basement. Her tears spilled down her cheeks and pattered onto the glass covering the wedding photo. They blurred the happy couple beyond recognition.

She could have done it. Both Amanda Layton and Josh Callahan undoubtedly wished she *had* done it. In the end Mary-

Margaret dropped the framed photo on the bed and walked into the bathroom with the straight razor.

She started on her hair with Ed's old razor. It was too dull and it hurt her scalp so she quickly switched to the small scissors in the medicine cabinet. Her locks fell into the sink and onto the floor and Mary-Margaret kept cutting. When she was finished she looked into the mirror. The woman staring back at her was unfamiliar. It was not just her hair but her eyes, as well. The woman smiled at her. Mary-Margaret knew what she was thinking. She returned the stranger's smile.

She took a shower and washed her hair and styled it in front of the mirror. She was in bed reading when Ed came home. She expected him to comment on her new hair style. She should have known better. He did not even look in her direction. He changed into his sweatpants and went back downstairs. He would return later and have his way with her. He was asleep moments after his discharge. Mary-Margaret continued reading for another thirty minutes before she turned off the light. It was best she got some sleep. Tomorrow was going to be a big day.

6.

Ed

She turned her head and smiled as her husband came inside through the garage. Her head still swam, pleasantly so, in fact, but Mary-Margaret put on what she hoped was a believable poker face. Ed, no stranger to being high himself, would notice nothing. In fact, he barely glanced up. He grumbled a "Hi, Mary-Margaret," on his way up the stairs.

Mary-Margaret sighed, replaced the magazine on the end table. She should have expected as much. Ed's usual routine of silence up to and through dinner was something to which she had grown accustomed over the years. On this day, for the first time since the day of their wedding, his silence worked to her advantage.

She got up quickly, found she could stand and walk without fear of tripping over her own feet. She was still high but she could handle it now. Either it was wearing off or she had gotten used to it. Either explanation would do. She made her way into the kitchen and started the spaghetti-in-clam-sauce. It was not among Ed's favorite dishes but he tolerated it. He knew how much she enjoyed it, and it seemed he had given in on that concession, if little else. When the water reached boil Mary-Margaret added the spaghetti and started on the sauce. She heard the toilet flush upstairs and Ed's heavy feet make their way to the bedroom. He would change into his sweatpants and a T-shirt and slip into his old, disgusting slippers. It was his preferred outfit for most nights, and she doubted this would be an exception.

Mary-Margaret arranged the dinner plates and the silverware. When dinner was ready she called up to her husband. Then she sat in her chair and waited.

Ed grimaced when he saw the meal that awaited him but he said nothing. The day's newspaper tucked under one arm he sat down and heaped half the spaghetti onto his plate. "Got a beer?"

Mary-Margaret smiled and stood and went to the fridge. She retrieved a beer and placed it in front of him. Then she filled her own plate and watched her husband. His movements reminded her of Josh, and the way he shoveled down the cereal earlier. In fact the resemblance was so strong Mary-Margaret's eyes went to the window looking out on the backyard. She quickly returned her attention to her dinner after a quick glance at Ed. She needn't have bothered; Ed either did not see her furtive glance outside or he simply did not care. Mary-Margaret ate her dinner in silence.

She thought of the needle-nose pliers she had taped beneath the tabletop in front of her. She had calculated the odds of this going down at the dinner table and decided the possibility was remote. She was pleased to be proved correct. They made for a lousy weapon, but they would do in a pinch. But they would not be needed, she knew that now. Ed was far too absorbed in his newspaper to even look in her direction. Even when he asked for seconds his nose remained buried in the sports section.

"Ed, how about some dinnertime conversation?" The sound of her voice surprised even her. It sounded too loud in the quiet kitchen.

Ed did not look up from his paper. Just as she was convinced he had not heard her, he said, "About what?" His voice, too, sounded odd, mostly because he rarely spoke at the table.

"I can tell you about my day at the office. It was somewhat eventful." *I fucked my boss and stared down the office manager. You should have seen the look on her face. It was fucking priceless.*

Ed shoveled more spaghetti into his mouth. His eyes never left the paper. He shrugged his shoulders.

Mary-Margaret thought again about the pliers. She could do it right now. He was so absorbed in whatever the Pirates had done last night he would have no idea what she was up to until it was done. But no. Not yet. It would be good but it would not be *Perfect.* She returned her attention to her plate.

"What the fuck did you do to your hair?"

The question startled Mary-Margaret. She jumped a little, mentally chastised herself. It was not the incredulous tone of Ed's voice, it was that he had asked a question to which she was completely unprepared to answer. She had planned a response the night before but it was gone from her mind. She tried to recall it but it remained missing from her mind. She stuttered.

"Looks like shit, Mary-Margaret. Christ, I can't stand short hair on women. What the fuck were you thinking?"

"I just wanted a change, darling," she replied. It was lame but it was all she had. It was also the truth. *That's why I fucked my boss and killed our son. Things had to change, Ed.* "It'll grow back if you really don't like it."

Ed frowned at her over the sports page. He shook his head and shoveled more spaghetti into his mouth. "Looks like shit," he repeated.

"I'm sorry."

They spent the rest of dinner in silence. When Ed was finished he stood and walked into the living room. Mary-Margaret helped herself to seconds—she was very hungry for some reason—and ate alone. When she was at last finished she stood and put her and Ed's plates into the sink.

The living room would work better than the kitchen. She had a garden trowel and a very large screwdriver hidden away. Either would work a little better than the pliers taped under the kitchen table.

She found Ed in the recliner, feet up, face still buried in the paper. The TV remote sat on the end table next to him. *Sports Center* was on, the talking heads going on about the coming weekend's Yankees/Red Sox series at Fenway. Ed hated both teams ("They spend all the money in the fucking world, and take our free agents away from us," was his usual complaint), which explained why he was not watching the TV. Once the announcers got off the Yankees and the Red Sox, Ed put the paper on his lap and returned his attention to the television.

Mary-Margaret sat on the sofa, at the end closest to her husband. The effects of the weed were finally gone. She found she missed the pleasant lightheadedness but she would not indulge again now even if Josh's pipe was still intact; she needed to be clear for the next few moments.

She picked up the remote and lowered the volume. Ed's head snapped in her direction. "You can't possibly tell me that was too loud."

"It wasn't, honey. I just wanted to talk for a minute."

"Can't it wait? I'm watching this." He reached for the remote.

She pulled it back. A mischievous smile spread across her lips. Her eyes flashed playfully.

Ed pursed his lips. "Mary-Margaret, what the fuck? Gimme the remote."

Mary-Margaret slipped the remote down inside her shirt. She leaned all the way back and puffed her chest. "Come and get it."

Ed hesitated, clearly unprepared for this. His eyes softened somewhat. His lips slowly turned up in what was a poor imitation of a smile. "What are you doing?" His voice was suddenly playful. For that split-second he was the man she married.

"Not to put too fine a point on it, Ed, but, hopefully, *you.*" She arched her back and purred.

Ed licked his lips. It was not a gesture of nervousness or even indecisiveness. It was lust, pure and simple. He probably did the same thing whenever he was about to fuck one of his lady friends. "What's gotten into you?" His tone was suspicious but excited.

Mr. Moore, murder, illegal substances, you name it. "Nothing. I just want to make love with my husband. Do I need a reason for that?"

Ed tossed the newspaper over his shoulder. The pages separated and fluttered to the floor. He licked his lips again. "Hell no."

He stood and Mary-Margaret could see his burgeoning erection through his sweats. He loomed over her, his eyes moving over every inch of her body. Her skin crawled under his examination. His hand reached down and brushed her shoulders, her breasts. Mary-Margaret cooed. She took the remote from under her shirt and tossed it onto the recliner.

Ed paid it no mind. He knelt beside the sofa. Saliva pooled at the corners of his lips and spilled out when he grinned again. He yanked down on Mary-Margaret's shirt suddenly and forcefully. The fabric tore, exposing her left breast. Ed fell upon her, kissing her chest. She felt his teeth brush the sensitive skin of her nipple. It sent small jolts of pain and pleasure throughout her body.

"Yes, Ed," she whispered. "Yes, baby." It felt good but not great. Mary-Margaret's exaggerated reaction had the desired effect. Her husband sucked on her nipple even harder. His right hand slipped under her shirt and massaged her other breast. Now she was getting somewhere.

Her hand slipped inside her jeans and found her clitoris. Her fingers massaged slowly, in rhythm with Ed's sucking and squeezing. She amazed herself when she realized she was close to orgasm. When it hit her she moaned loudly. Her muscles contracted, forcing Ed to bear down on her breasts. Mary-Margaret climaxed even more powerfully than she had with Moore. The power of her orgasm robbed her of breath and drove all thought from her mind. As the tremors subsided she breathed heavily and hugged Ed.

"I assume Josh isn't home," he muttered.

Mary-Margaret muttered breathlessly. "No."

"Then what are we waiting for?" He tore off his shirt and stripped off his sweats. As she had already seen, Ed sported a full erection. He plopped down on the sofa next to her. "Suck it, baby."

Mary-Margaret smiled conspiratorially. "I thought you'd never ask." As Ed invaded her mouth she made mental comparisons to Mr. Moore. Her husband was not as big or as wide but it was still pleasurable to wrap her lips around him. She could not remember the last time she had had any real sexual contact with Ed. Years, certainly. She half-expected to taste another woman on his penis but it seemed today he had foregone any of his other lovers. It would have made no difference to Mary-Margaret; her Perfect Day allowed for either scenario.

Ed lay back with his eyes closed and his hand on the back of her head. He groaned his approval, every few moments adding a mumbled, "Yeah, baby", undoubtedly meant to encourage her. Mary-Margaret needed no encouragement. This was something she wanted to do, *needed* to do, in order for her day to be Perfect.

After several more moments she slowed and then stopped. She looked up at her husband. "Fuck me, Ed. Fuck me right now."

He shoved her off the sofa. She landed on her knees and barely contained her surprised yelp. Ed jumped off the sofa and stood behind her. He pushed her forward until she was bent over the sofa. He dropped to his knees behind her and placed his hands on her hips.

"Yes, Ed. *Yes.*"

Ed penetrated her roughly. He made up for any physical shortfalls with powerful thrusts that drove him deep inside her. Mary-Margaret moaned, mostly with pain but there might have been the merest fraction of pleasure, as well. Most of the times she had sex with Ed, back when they did have sex, it ended with her unfulfilled. This, as in everything else that had happened today, might be different.

It might have been the thought of her dead son buried in the backyard. It might also have been the knowledge that, one way or another, this was the last time she would ever be with Ed. The idea made her smile despite the painful thrusting of her husband. Incredibly, she felt her orgasm starting to build. Four in one day? Mary-Margaret felt it and welcomed it.

The orgasm hit and this time she screamed. Moving purely on instinct, she reached behind her and shoved Ed back. She heard him gasp even over the pounding in her ears.

"Holy shit, Mary-Margaret!"

Ed did not move, did not touch her. He seemed content to gape at the display before him. The orgasm wracked her body for another moment before the tremors started to fade. Mary-Margaret breathed heavily, her face half-buried in the sofa cushions. "God...God..."

"Oh, fuck yeah!" Ed sounded both amazed and ecstatic. He entered her again quite viciously, slamming himself deeper inside her. "That's the way I like it!"

Mary-Margaret recovered slowly. The force of her orgasm had drained her. It took several moments for her to simply lift her head from the sofa. Her arms and legs shook. Slowly, she caught her breath. With her senses recovered she became aware that Ed was still there, still plowing her from behind. Mary-Margaret reached behind her and grabbed her husband's ass and directed his rhythm, slowing him down enough that the pain left her.

She remembered the trowel she had hidden beneath the sofa, almost directly in front of her. She smiled. Judging by Ed's thrusts and breathing, he was getting closer to orgasm. That would most likely result in him cumming on her back, maybe her ass. He was not there yet but he could see the finish line. Mary-Margaret's smile widened. "Cum in my mouth, Ed. I want to *taste* it."

"God*damn*, baby," he gasped. "What's up with you today?"

"Less talk, more cum."

He picked up the pace, slamming himself deeper inside her and driving her face into the sofa cushions. Mary-Margaret gasped for air, still out of breath from her last orgasm and finding it difficult to breathe in her current position. If he did not finish soon she may pass out, and that was definitely *not* part of her plan.

"I want it, Ed. I *need* it." At first she thought he simply did not hear her. He was breathing heavy and groaning and her voice was muffled by the damned cushions. She felt his pace accelerating even more and she thought, *Christ, he's gonna cum inside me. Then what do I do?*

His pace continued to quicken. With a strangled moan he pulled out of her. Mary-Margaret picked up her head and gulped air. She had time for only one deep breath before she turned and opened her mouth wide to receive her husband.

Ed grabbed the back of her head and shoved his penis into her mouth. Mary-Margaret felt the first hot shot of ejaculate hit the back of her mouth.

Then she bit down with all the force she could muster.

The first thing that happened was the salty taste of her husband's seed mingled with the coppery taste of his blood. It mixed together into a viscous broth and filled her mouth and slid down her throat.

The second thing that happened, one millisecond after the first, was Ed screamed. He was momentarily frozen in place, obviously unable to figure out what just happened. As the pain center of his brain lit up like a Christmas tree he jerked backward, away from her.

Mary-Margaret bit down as hard as she was able, clamping her teeth together in a bear trap. She felt the insides of her husband's penis struggle to keep the thing in one piece. She used all her teeth to saw and grind through the veins and meat of Ed's still-hard penis.

He screamed again and this time he took a step closer to her. His hands found her head and he felt about like a blind man. His scream turned into gibberish which she could not understand, no doubt pleading with her.

Mary-Margaret bit down again and finished the job.

Ed backpedaled and lost his balance. He landed on his ass ten feet from her. Blood fountained from the inch or two of penis he still possessed. Some landed on his chest, his arms, in his hair. One hand grasped his ruined manhood and he looked at it with eyes bugged and mouth agape.

Mary-Margaret rose to her knees. She could feel the thing softening in her mouth. She considered swallowing it but the thought of any part of Ed lingering inside her body was simply too much for her. She turned her head and spat it onto the hardwood. It rolled a few inches before it came to a stop next to Ed's discarded shirt.

She felt the blood/semen mixture dribble down her chin. Some of it was still in her mouth and she spat again. The taste of his cum was gone, overwhelmed by the blood that somehow managed to find its way down her throat despite her efforts. It coated her teeth and her tongue, it dripped from her chin. She spat again. "That was quite a load you managed, Ed."

Ed sat on the floor, both hands now holding and covering the stub that used to be his pride and joy. He whispered, "Oh, Jesus, oh, Jesus, oh, Jesus." Sweat coated his face, his arms; it mixed with the blood from those first few spurts.

Mary-Margaret used the sofa to push herself to her feet. Her legs shook, probably from a combination of her world-shattering orgasm and what she had just done to her husband. Her arms shook as well and she could feel her heart slamming the inside of her ribcage. She took an unsteady step in her husband's direction.

Ed ignored her. He was focused entirely on the remains of his penis. His hands no longer curled around the base, most likely because it had shrunk away to almost nothing. Instead they were pressed against the stump. Blood flowed freely between his fingers; there was already a sizeable pool of it on the floor between his legs. "Oh, Jesus, oh, Jesus," he continued.

Mary-Margaret scooped up Ed's shirt and wiped her chin. The shirt came away bloody. She was surprised at how bright the blood appeared. It was nearly neon in the semi-darkened living room. She dabbed at the corners of her mouth, spat into the shirt, and dropped it to her side.

Ed had switched to "Holy fuck, holy fuck," while she cleaned herself. His eyes remained focused with laser intensity at the gore originating from where his penis used to be. The rest of the world, Mary-Margaret included, had ceased to exist for the moment.

"Ed, Josh is dead. I poisoned him and buried him in the backyard. Just FYI, honey."

Ed did not look up. He did not respond at all.

"You should have seen him go. And you call *me* a pussy."

Ed continued staring at the ruins of his manhood. At last her words must have penetrated the fog that obscured the rest of the world. He looked up at her, blankly. He blinked a few times, his mouth worked, but he seemed incapable of speech.

Mary-Margaret began wiping at the few droplets of her husband's blood that landed on her. Most of it was on her chest and her arms and she used her husband's shirt to clean herself. "He's gone, Ed. I buried him in the backyard near the tree line. I'm gonna get some seeds and plant nice flowers over his grave. Just thought you should know that."

Ed stared dumbly at her. Blood continued to seep between his fingers. The pool in which he sat continued to expand, reaching and flowing around the shrunken ruin that used to do all his thinking for him.

Mary-Margaret continued cleaning herself. "I thought you'd be happy, darling. You never wanted Josh, anyway. We both know that. Now you don't have to worry about him, anymore. He's out of the picture."

"Mary-Margaret..." A microbe of awareness crept into his eyes. His hands remained in his lap, his mouth remained agape, but his eyes were no longer completely blank. "Mary-Margaret..."

Mary-Margaret finished cleaning her husband's blood from her skin. His shirt fell from her fingers and landed half-inside the spreading puddle of Ed's blood. She reached down and retrieved her shirt. She pulled it on over her head, noting with satisfaction her limbs no longer threatened to shake themselves free of her torso. Her heart was still beating much too quickly, and her breathing was fast, but she felt calmer than she had since her brief meeting with Josh's marijuana.

"What's wrong, darling?" Her voice was tender, loving. "Oh, I get it. You're not used to speaking to me anymore. It has been a long time, after all. Well, that's okay, Ed. I still love you."

Ed blinked at her again. His eyes fell on the sad, shriveled remains of his penis. Keeping one hand covering the stump he got to his knees and pulled himself along the floor toward it. His breath hitched as he inched along the floor. He dragged himself across the widest part of the puddle of gore, leaving streaks in his wake. His eyes remained focused on the severed organ.

Mary-Margaret did not move, simply looked down and smiled at the man she promised to honor and cherish for the rest of her life. "That might work, Ed. They might be able to reattach your cock if you get to a hospital in time." She strode forward and then slammed her foot down on the object that a few moments ago brought her such pleasure. She felt the pathetic thing deflate beneath her foot. It made an odd squishy sound Mary-Margaret had never before heard.

"*NO!*" Ed scrambled the rest of the way. He clawed feebly at Mary-Margaret's foot, trying to lift it from the floor. "Nononononono."

Mary-Margaret twisted her foot as if demonstrating a dance move. Ed moaned and continued his feeble attempt to move his wife's foot. Then, quite slowly and with great satisfaction, Mary-Margaret did the job herself. She stepped back and allowed her husband some room.

Ed picked up the flattened and bloody piece of flesh. He cradled it in his free hand and whimpered.

"You fucked your last floozy, Ed. And you fucked me for the last time, too. Although in the spirit of giving credit where due, that last time was one for the ages. I'll remember that one for a long time, so you should be proud of yourself, honey."

Ed crawled to the recliner and used it to push himself to his feet. His feet slipped a bit in the pool of blood but he kept his balance. He did not even look in Mary-Margaret's direction. Instead he stumbled for the kitchen. "Dr. Perry," he whispered. "I need Dr. Perry. His number's above the phone, right? I think it is." He penguin-walked toward the kitchen. Blood pattered on the floor behind him.

Mary-Margaret followed her husband casually, arms folded across her chest. "You may as well call Katy Perry, for all the good a doctor's gonna do you, babe." She was careful to sidestep the trail of blood left in her husband's wake as she entered the kitchen.

Ed's hand shook when he reached for the phone. Blood dripped from his fingers and the phone slipped from his grasp. It hit the floor and the battery hatch popped off and skipped across the linoleum. Ed dropped down to his knees and fumbled for the phone.

Mary-Margaret leaned in the doorway, arms still folded, and regarded her husband with amusement. "Would you like to be buried next to our son? It's backbreaking work, digging a grave, but I wouldn't mind, if that's what you want."

Ed landed two fingers on the phone but it skittered away. He was trembling now and his movements became slow and sluggish. He plopped down into a seated position, both hands now held against the bloody mess that used to be his nether regions. He looked at his wife with blank eyes. "Mary-Margaret."

"Yes, dear?" Mary-Margaret left the doorway and stood before her husband. She knelt in front of him, looked into his eyes.

Ed's lips trembled. He mumbled something. Mary-Margaret leaned in closer.

The dying light in Ed's eyes blazed to full intensity quite suddenly. The pathetic wretch he had become since Mary-Margaret relieved him of his manhood vanished and the old Ed was back. Mary-Margaret had time to recognize the change but not to get out of the way. Ed's right hand shot from his groin and his fingers wrapped themselves around her throat.

Mary-Margaret gasped and instinctively pulled away. Ed's fingers slipped off her neck when he tried to squeeze her throat. Mary-Margaret fell back, coughing and rubbing her neck. Ed lunged after her. He landed on top and his sudden weight exploded the breath from her lungs. His hands found her throat again and he clamped down hard. Mary-Margaret kicked her legs and squirmed beneath her husband's bulk. His fingers, slick with blood, nonetheless found purchase around her throat.

"You're gonna die, bitch! You're gonna die and the cops will give me a fucking medal. Psycho twat kills her own son and maims her husband. I bet even your cunt friends in the office will say you deserved this."

Mary-Margaret struggled against the hands at her throat. Bright pinpricks of light began to dance at the edges of her vision. *Stupid stupid stupid. Got overconfident, Mary-Margaret. How are you gonna get out of this one?* Quickly she reached down into the mess that used to be Ed's groin and dug her fingers into something wet and hot. Ed screamed and Mary-Margaret winced. She drove her fingers and then her entire hand into the wound. Hot blood splashed her arm up to her elbow. Ed howled and threw himself off of her.

Mary-Margaret rolled away, coughing and rubbing her throat. She gulped air in great whooping gasps. Her other hand, the one not covered with her husband's blood, wiped at the tears in her eyes. *Get up, Mary-Margaret. Get up before* he *does.* She felt blindly for the counter and found it was directly in front of her. Mary-Margaret used it to pull herself to her feet. Her legs shook but she willed them to keep her upright. She wiped at more tears until she could open her eyes.

Ed was in the corner of the kitchen, lying on his side and curled into a ball. The pool of blood around him widened but he seemed oblivious to it. His body shook violently. Weak moans reached her ears.

Mary-Margaret stutter-stepped to the kitchen table. She groped about beneath the tabletop, her fingers probing for the pliers. "I admit I got a little overconfident. I won't make that mistake again, Ed. No fucking way, baby." Her fingers closed around the handle and she tore the thing loose from the tape securing it to the underside of the table. She held it like a dagger and approached her husband.

Ed looked lazily at her. Saliva and blood dripped from his lips to the linoleum. He took a shuddering breath. "Help me, Mary-Margaret." His voice quavered, his whole body shook.

"Of course, Ed."

7.

Denouement

The rain started shortly after 9:30. Mary-Margaret dragged her husband's corpse into the backyard. She plopped him in front of the fresh mound of earth that covered their son's body. After she retrieved the shovel she went back to work. The rain served to soften the ground and that was a big help. Even so, by the time the hole was dug her muscles were screaming and her hands were blistered and sore.

It was a struggle to drag Ed's body to the edge of the hole. She sank to her knees and shoved the corpse with everything she had left. Ed tumbled into the hole and settled face-down in the dirt. Mary-Margaret nearly fell in after him. She caught herself at the last moment and managed to throw herself to the side of the grave. There she lay, eyes closed and chest heaving, the rain washing the blood and sweat from her clothes and her body. She might have passed out if not for the throbbing in her arms and legs.

Several moments later she used the shovel to pull herself to her feet. Then she filled in the dirt around her husband's naked body. The shovel was slippery from both the rain and the blood from the popped blisters on her hands. It took much longer to cover Ed than it had to make Josh vanish from the face of the earth. Exhausted to the point of collapse Mary-Margaret dropped the shovel and staggered toward the house.

The kitchen was still a wreck. It would have to wait. She was far too tired and sore to deal with that. The copious amounts of Ed's blood and other bodily fluids would keep until morning. She would have to bathe, of course; there was no way she was getting blood and mud on her clean sheets. She ran the bath and stepped into the tub when it was ready.

Whether she fell asleep or passed out the end result was the same.

Mary-Margaret dreamed of what her life should have been. She and Ed, deeply in love and together, their relationship based on respect and truth. There were no floozies in this version, no alcohol beyond the occasional bottle of wine by the fireplace. Josh was the model child who did well in school and loved his parents unconditionally. She was back to working in the book store and she enjoyed her mornings before she rushed home to take care of her family. Unconscious or asleep in the tub, Mary-Margaret smiled.

She awoke still smiling. The water in the tub was lukewarm at best. Her fingers were pruned. Mary-Margaret shivered and reached for her towel. She dried off quickly but she was still cold. Back in her bedroom she pulled on her pajamas quickly and threw on her robe and cinched the tie closed. "Maybe a cup of tea," she announced. "Just one before bed."

She was downstairs in the kitchen again a moment later. It was still a wreck, the floor and walls still decorated with her late husband's blood. Mary-Margaret was careful not to step into any of the puddles and streaks with her slippers. She stood by the stove and waited for the kettle to whistle and then poured herself a cup of tea. She evacuated the kitchen, finding it too filthy and depressing to remain a moment longer.

Her next choice was the living room. More of Ed's bodily fluids stained the floors and walls, the furniture. Mary-Margaret had failed to notice—to *really* notice—just how much blood had escaped from her husband's body during those first Perfect moments. In here the blood was thick, congealing. Mary-Margaret frowned and took her tea upstairs to the bedroom.

She got under the blankets and lay there with her eyes closed for several moments. The house was quiet, as quiet as it had been since they moved in. Mary-Margaret listened to the silence and let it wash over her like a warm breeze. "Should have done this years ago," she said to the empty bedroom. "Why did I wait so long?" She nearly nodded off, but she wanted to savor the last few hours of the Perfect Day.

Eventually she sat up in bed and sipped her tea and read her novel. When her eyes grew heavy she put the book on the nightstand and turned off the light.

She lay in the darkness, listening to her own breathing, her own heartbeat. The wind outside picked up a bit and pressed against the windows.

"It'll never get better than today," she whispered.

The statement caused her breath to catch in her throat. It was as if someone else had entered the room and whispered into her ear. Her eyes flew open. She could see the silhouette of the ceiling fan above her and the shadows of trees on the walls. Her heart suddenly picked up the pace.

The voice was correct, of course. Whatever she did with the rest of her life she would never again experience a day as Perfect as this one. The thought had come from nowhere and now it dominated her. *Never again, Mary-Margaret. It's all downhill from here.*

She was still high from her Perfect Day but she could sense the euphoria starting to slip. "No," she whispered. She could deny it but she knew the realization was correct. She lay in the darkness of her bedroom and knew she could never again be this happy, this content.

Her arm shot for the lamp and she succeeded in knocking the alarm clock and her book off the nightstand. Desperate, her heart racing, Mary-Margaret tried again for the lamp. She succeeded and harsh light flooded the bedroom. She blinked at its assault and rolled onto Ed's side. She pawed clumsily at the drawer to his nightstand. It seemed stuck—although she knew it was not—and it took her several attempts to open it.

Ed's nine millimeter was hidden beneath some hardcore porn magazines he had long since stopped hiding from her. She had left it in place on the off-chance she and Ed made it in here before she could deal with him. She grasped for it, felt her fingers close around the handle. She withdrew the ugly, cold thing and looked at it.

Her head swam, her eyes focused on Ed's "intruder welcoming device." She became aware her breath was coming in giant gulps of air.

"Today was perfect," she said, nearly out of breath. Her heart hammered away within her chest. She closed her eyes and pictured the look on Amanda Layton's face when Mary-Margaret finally turned the tables on her. She thought of Mr. Moore (*God damn, Mary-Margaret, you're full of surprises today.*) and the office sofa upon which her Perfect Day had truly begun. She pictured Josh and his pathetic mewling just before he shit himself and died. And Ed. Every detail of Ed's last moments played in vivid HD behind her eyes.

Life will never be as good as it is at this moment. It will never be Perfect *again.*

Tears trickled down her cheeks. She sniffled. She did not know it but she was smiling quite broadly. "Today really was a Perfect Day."

Mary-Margaret placed the nine millimeter against her temple.

About the Authors

Elizabeth Alsobrooks

Her adult children still shiver in MI, but Elizabeth enjoys the sunny Sonoran Desert where she lives with her personal editor, Hudson (AKA Maltese), and husband, Kenton, (AKA Irish-Scotsman) at the foot of the beautiful Santa Catalina Mountain Range where she writes Urban Fantasy, Horror, and nonfiction. She is currently working on the next book in her **Illuminati** series and is collaborating with a photo-graphic artist on a Tarot deck and accompanying manuals that coordinate with the mythology and symbolism behind her Illuminati series. Keep up with her and her novels on her website, blog and social media sites:

www.elizabethalsobrooks.com

Joseph J Christiano

Joe grew up in Connecticut's Naugatuck Valley. A voracious reader since he was old enough to hold a book in his hands, he surprised his second grade teacher by using the word "invulnerable" (learned from a Superman comic book) in a sentence. He wrote his first story at the ripe old age of 11. His published works include the novels *Dark Annie, Old Ghosts, and The Shadowman.* His favorite authors and influences include Richard Matheson, Rod Sterling, Agatha Christie, Stephen King, Alan Moore and Neil Gaiman. You can follow him at: https://www.facebook.com/JosephJChristiano/

Daniel Hunter

Daniel grew up and lived in the Great Northwest. Throughout his younger years, his two greatest passions were storytelling and aviation. His first great adventure led him into the United States Air Force after college. Countless states, countries, and continents later, he moved to the Southeastern part of the United States after leaving the Air Force. He still finds himself in the world of travel while continuing to spend time with his family and write stories in his time of leisure.

Robert James

Tell-Tale's 2015 Winner of the Vincent Price Award! Robert James is an emerging author of dark fantasy, horror, and supernatural thrillers. A former history teacher, he ran screaming from the classroom into a career in public policy. His stories draw on his love for Great Lakes maritime history, his worst fears, and the Irish chip on his shoulder. When he's not padding his resume for dad of the year, you'll catch him listening to anything from acoustic folk to death metal, reading about the mysteries of the universe, or playing guitar. Everyone has demons. Escape yours at:

http://www.RJfiction.com

Patricia Mattern

Patricia along with coauthors J. C. Estall & M. Mattern are the Award-Winning, Amazon #1 and Top 100 Bestselling authors of the Full Moon Series, Strident House, Shock of Night, Andy of the Damned, Forest of Bleeding Trees, Vampire Princess, Fangirl (with Danielle James) and more. She began composing stories in utero and was born with a stylus clutched in her tiny hand. She relies on her background as a Behavioral Specialist to add depth to her characters and is currently involved with one of them ("It's complicated."). Patricia is a member of the Thriller Writers Association & Erotic Authors Guild. Connect with Patricia at her website and social media:

https://www.facebook.com/P-Mattern-334553956700450/

Tell-Tale Publishing would like to thank you for your purchase. If you would like to read more from these or other TT authors, please visit our website: http://www.tell-talepublishing.com